Clairvoyant

A Novel

Devan Arntson

Clairvoyant

ISBN: 978-0-578-22465-7

To Troop 84 of Proctor, Minnesota
And to the Brothers I found there

Clairvoyant

Contents

Prologue

Book One: Clairvoyant

Book Two: Homeaiming

Book Three: Redemption

Prologue

I think that I chose the title, *Clairvoyant*, for a number of reasons. Foremostly, I couldn't come up with anything better. I whimsically named the book when I first started writing it. So, through laziness and lack of any good ideas, the name stuck. Though as it happens, I believe it works well with the story as it evolved, covering the whole range of definitions the word, *Clairvoyant*, takes on.

The word itself is most often used to describe the false appearance of knowledge or the people who think they have all the answers. It seemed fitting for a story about a group of teenage boys, who tend to think they know what's best. I believe it also works well with the mystery overtones of the first act, as the characters search and strive to have all the answers.

The first time I heard the word, it was in reference to the ability of always knowing where to go. I thought this was especially appropriate for the second act of the book, being that the characters are set in their plan and direction. It seemed that the adventurers always knew exactly where they were headed. Even as they went into the unknown, they were confident in their course.

Yet as I wrote, I soon realized that in order to have an adventure, you can never know where you are going. So then, the title becomes something ironic. Adventure can only take place as soon as you're off the map, as soon as you go somewhere that you didn't plan for. In the last act, this concept is explored more as the characters are taken by the forces of the world, to places they never imagined.

Even as I was writing the story, I wrote things I never expected. I had every intention of stopping after the first act, because the book was simply meant to be something fun for my Boy Scout troop, whose various stories and tall tales are now immortalized in the pages to follow. Yet as I aged out of the Scouts and all of my friends began drifting into their own lives away from each other, I realized that the story needed to continue. One man's life isn't defined by one period of time, it keeps going. Sometimes stretching a man's battle over years and decades.

This book that I've been chipping away at for five years now, has evolved and taken me on an adventure I never knew I would go on. I can only hope and pray that you will find the same adventure; if not within the pages of a book, then out in the world.

Book One
Clairvoyant

Clairvoyant

First Days

I hadn't been in camp five minutes, the time I found the body. It had washed up along the shore of Long Lake. The corpse, face down, brushed against the weeds with the ebb and flow of the water. The cops were notified not long after. They came into our camp, identified, and took the boy away. I don't remember if I was the one who called for them, or if it was one of the adults. Bloody water streamed from his battered body, as the flesh on his limbs was torn nearly off the bone. The searing image of a dead boy was the only thing I remember from that moment.

I had to be there when the officials talked to the camp counselors; though I stood in back and didn't say a word. For whatever reason it was agreed upon that night, Camp Tomahawk should continue as scheduled that week. Mourning never came. It haunted me all summer and probably for the rest of my life. I couldn't escape it, even after camp ended. It's all I thought about; all I dreamt about. The question remained in my mind, "who killed Jay Edgar?"

I walked back on the dark trail to the campsite. My scoutmaster wanted to stay in the head building and continue to ask as many questions as the deputies were willing to answer. From what I heard; they weren't willing to give any. I wasn't in favor of staying at camp that week, but it became something that I would have to live with.

The guys were still up and waiting for me when I got back to the nest. The younger scouts were sent off to their tents as soon as the adults heard the news about the body. The restless middle schoolers were probably going crazy in the confined space.

I don't know what it was, but adults had it programmed into them to try relentlessly to shelter children from death as long as possible. The older boys were allowed to stay out, though. I suppose the chaperons figured us juniors and seniors could handle topics like death. They sat around the fire and only raised their eyes when they saw me sit down on the log next to them. Rick, one of my friends, nudged me with his elbow, causing me to meet his dark eyes.

"You good?" He asked softly, barely louder than the crack of the fire. I looked at him and nodded silently. No other words were spoken, but the silence did more for us than talking about the elephant in the room. We didn't have anything to say, so we sat there in reverence and disbelief.

As dawn came closer, the guys, one by one, went to bed. Rick left last. He put his hand on my shoulder to comfort me as he went to our tent that we would be sharing that week. The stars that just peeked through the trees faded as the pale sky came into being. The scouts were up and getting ready for breakfast and there I was, still staring at the pile of ash that had stopped smoking hours ago. I heard from behind me that one of the adult leaders wanted to come talk to me, but someone stopped them.

"Just leave him be. The boys will reach him better than we could." Sighed our scoutmaster, Richard Senior, who was Rick's dad. In a way, he was a father figure to all the guys. We all grew up in this troop and he had always been there for us. He knew how to teach us life lessons, even when we really messed up and I'd always respect him for that.

"Hey Lane!" It was another member of our gang, Zeke, calling for me. I turned around, to see him toss me a pack of oatmeal. "I know you're still hungry!" He wasn't wrong. Those morning meals when it was still cold outside, and we made piping hot oatmeal, were honestly the best. Hot cinnamon burned in my belly like a warm hearth. We sat haphazardly around the picnic bench as we ate. Zeke and Rick were there with me, as well as Jack, Joe, and Allan, the rest of our established clique.

"So, what are we gonna do?" Zeke openly asked the crew as he fixed his honey tea.

"Uh, what do you mean?" Joe chuckled as he poked his food.

"Don't you guys wanna know what happened, why he was there?" Everyone at the table snapped at him to shut up. "I'm serious, I want to find out and I know you do too," he turned to me.

"Honestly just let the cops take care of it," Joe was very much the voice of reason in our group. Whenever Zeke would get a wild idea, Joe would tell him how improbable it was. The rest of us would usually come up with a middle-ground solution that was still outlandish but well thought-out. This was the delicate balance that our crew operated in. We ran a tight ship, no matter what we were doing.

"Zeke's right," I spoke up.

"Wait what?" Jack turned to me.

"I wanna know what happened to the boy. But I have no idea how we would ever find out on our own."

"You wouldn't," Joe shook his head, his thin wire glasses slowly falling down his husky face. "He was in the lake for God knows how long, so there wouldn't be any evidence left of what happened."

"Ah, shit," Jack popped up from his lawn chair that was at the end of the table, interrupting the conversation at hand. "We gotta get ready for morning colors," We turned and saw the other scouts assembling around the flagpole.

"Yeah we should probably get cleaned up," We all pushed off from the worn table, it creaked and rocked as we moved about it. Some say this was the first table made in the Midwest, left behind from the voyagers, and I would strongly agree based on its broken condition.

I walked with Rick to our quarters. It was built up from the forest on a wooden platform and was a military green, canvas tent. Same as any in Camp Tomahawk. They peeked through the brush below like an army of tree houses.

"You really thinking about trying to solve this?" He stopped me as I was tucking my khaki shirt into the olive uniform pants. "Zeke seems pretty bent on having us do this."

"It's not even Ezekiel's issue," I snapped hastily. "If he's willing to help, fine, but this isn't for him. He didn't see what I saw."

"Don't isolate yourself on this, besides he isn't the only one who wants to help."

"You too, huh?" I looked over at him, who was sitting on his cot, tying his crimson red neckerchief around his neck, which he usually wore as a bandana.

"I know this means something to you, and I'd be lying if I said I wasn't a little curious. Everyone is. So, don't get in your head that this is your crusade alone. Sure, you saw the corpse up close and it was haunting, but don't make this more personal than his family is."

"You're right. I'm sorry," I sighed. "I don't know what Zeke has in mind, but right now we gotta lay low. Honestly, maybe just ask the counselors if they've heard anything or know anything we don't.

During our free time today, I may sneak over to the registration building, see if they have a newspaper."

"Ok, I'll ask around," He nodded. Rick was lean, but surprisingly strong. Years of cross country running kept him slim. He had buzzed brown hair, which mirrored his future aspirations of serving in the Marines.

We walked out of the dusty tent and made way to where Zeke and Allan were lining up in our patrol. Our troop was comprised of several patrols, my gang of six made up one of them. Every patrol had a flag and war cry of its own. We fashioned a red banner with an arrow on fire, embroidered in yellow. As boys, we made this flag and formed this patrol when we all first joined the scouts, and it has since been a token of our comradery.

Zeke could be seen from a mile away, he was small in frame, but his thick, curly brown hair stuck out amongst the crowd. However, our attention was caught by something else. A first-year scout was standing like a statue, staring at the cove, where just yesterday I had found the corpse. We walked up to him; his daunted expression never changed.

"They told us to stay in our tents," He turned with his white face to us. "But I didn't know why. I went out j-just to have a peek."

"Oh shit. How long have you been out here?" I asked softly, knowing he had been paralyzed all night.

"He was right there," The boy broke down and started bawling. He went and clung onto Rick, whether he wanted a hug or not. We took the young scout up to the fire ring, where most everyone communed.

"Dad," Rick called for our scoutmaster in a serious voice. He turned from his cup of coffee and came over to see the young boy still in tears.

"What happened?" He asked us sternly as he knelt down in front of the kid.

"He said he saw the cops take the body away. Seemed to have really gotten to him," I responded. He grabbed the kid's shoulder and led him presumably to the nurse. We could see that Richard was talking to him as they went up the trail.

"What was that about?" Joe came up from behind us, tucking in his uniform. We proceeded to tell him. I saw the whole thing happen right in front of me, so I can only imagine what the sixth grader was going through.

The other adults still had us line up for morning colors. We all gave the scout salute as the American flag was raised, with the red and green, Troop 84 banner to follow.

"Pledge of Allegiance," The color guard commander called out. We chanted the pledge to our country. Though the high flag couldn't be seen by anyone under the brims of our campaign hats.

"Scout Oath," The salute moved to the ninety-degree scout sign.

"On my honor, I will do my best, to do my duty to God and my country. To obey the scout law. To help other people at all times. To keep myself physically strong, mentally awake, and morally straight," The assembly echoed in reply.

"Law."

"A scout is trustworthy, loyal, helpful, friendly, courteous, kind, obedient, cheerful, thrifty, brave, clean, and reverent!" We hollered.

"Dismissed!"

After colors, everyone dispersed for their merit badges. Zeke and I had Wilderness Survival. We went through one of countless trails that meandered through camp to get to Scoutcraft, where the class would meet. Now Scoutcraft was every boys' dream. It was built by the older scouts who worked at camp over the years. Using only rope and cut down logs, they had built a complex jungle gym high up in the trees. Every year, at least one scout would break their arm on the monkey bars alone. Not even to mention the tractor-tire swing or the forty-foot tightrope.

We gathered at the man-made spiderweb. There wasn't enough room for everyone, so those who came late had to attend class from the ground among the bugs and ticks. The instructor, I could tell, started talking to the ten of us that took the course. Yet, I didn't hear a single word he said. I stared off into the deep of the woods, a ghostly fog sifted between the emerald pines.

"He's out there," I whispered as I turned to Zeke. "I feel it. I don't know, I just feel like we're not safe."

"I don't know, maybe Joe's right. How do we know it wasn't natural causes?" He pipped back.

"I saw the body up close; it was mutilated. Which means there's a *mutilator* somewhere out there. Not to sound grizzly, but that's what happened."

"We have nothing to go off of. Yes, I want to help, but thinking on it, how could we know what happened or who did it?"

"The town is too small for anyone to hide, but *this* is a big place. He could be right here in camp. There's a lot of uncharted woods here for someone to hide."

"Boys!" The counselor snapped at us. "Are any of you paying attention?"

"Yup," I said dully without hesitation.

"Ok, good. So, going back to the Outdoor Code..."

"I'm gonna go to the registration building during lunch to see if anyone there has heard any updates," I continued to Zeke.

Later, our troop would meet up in camp and march to the dining hall together. I was kicking myself for sneaking away from the meal. Camp food always tasted good, but I needed to get any info I could.

"If anyone asks where I am, I ate a bad patch of frogs and will be in the latrine for a while," Teens were hustling about the mess hall, so I passed unnoticed on my way out. I could still hear the assemblage of boys shouting from over the hill. All the guys at camp ate there, with the exception of the higher up officials who ran the camp, who were served on fancy platters, and those poor sods a mile away at the horse corral.

The road to this registration building was a couple miles. It was hot and dusty; with each step, a small cloud would form beneath my feet. The road was a stripe of desert in the middle of the forest biome. The heat radiated off the dirt and it didn't help that I hadn't cared to bring water. I kept a reasonable pace, though I wasn't too worried about making time, there were never any scheduled events right after lunch anyway.

Getting out of the grove, there was a clearing of where they put in a golf course. For the wealthy visitors, I guess. I never seen any scouts use it. I cut through there to save some distance. The registration center would be right over the hill as opposed to walking the long way on the road. It was large and overly fancy. Before it, was the rock-climbing tower and the high ropes course which were basically for show since they were also lightly used. Walking inside the glass double doors, I was welcomed by the gods' gift of air conditioning. A decently round man at the desk didn't seem to avert his attention to my entrance, he sat back in his chair and read some aged book. I walked up to him, nonetheless.

"Do you guys have any newspapers?" He raised his eyes just barely over the tops of the pages to meet me.

"Let me go check," He sighed as he sat up from where was reclining. Waddling farther behind the counter, he pulled out a stack of local newspapers that he hadn't cared to open yet. He went straight back to his chair, which I couldn't figure out how it held him up. I cut the twine that held the papers together and went for the top one. As I sat myself down on the nearest bench, I scanned the cover for anything relevant. Nothing. After flipping through the pages of weather and ads, I came to the very back. Among the obituaries of several elderly people in the county, the young boy stuck out.

> Jay Edgar, 15, died 16th July 1972 in Long Lake, after drowning from a swimming accident. His body was recovered yesterday in Tomahawk Scout Reservation. He was raised in Nobleton, WI and lived there all his life. He is survived by his aunt and legal guardian, Darlene Edgar. No public funeral will be held.

I didn't want to believe it. I couldn't. I saw the body only a few feet away. There were bruises on his spine and cuts on his limbs. "Jesus Christ, what happened to him?" Were the words spoken by the first responder. It made me angry that the cops fed the press some petty story. I was no detective, but I know for a fact that it wasn't an accident. It consumed me to think that something was being hidden. Just the thought that a kid had just been murdered a few days before and the police are making it out to be some random incident. They put no thought into what happened and that sickened me. I tossed the paper back on the counter on my way out.

I hung my head as I walked back to camp, hearing nothing but the crunch of the rocks with each step I took. The red neckerchief around my neck got a little dustier. The sun beat down on me with its fierce heat. I was angry, something deep down told me that it was my responsibility to find out exactly what happened. I didn't know the boy, Jay, but he and I were now connected. His soul leeched onto me and feed on my ambition to find his murderer.

That night I crashed; I went to bed significantly earlier than anyone else. I was so tired, and it all caught up to me in the null of events. Not that I slept well, though. I saw him, wading out in the lake and just standing there. It was night and the only sound was the gentle bump in the waves meeting the boys' legs. His face, though hardly visible, was expressionless. He stared through me with a chilling gaze. He could see into me, he knew who I was, knew everything about me. But he just stood there judging me. "Who are you to have found me?" His figure would seem to say. I turned around. Now in front of me, a monstrous figure stood over me. I tripped over a root and rolled backwards into the lake. As I scrambled to get myself up, my hand touched another. It was the now lifeless body of the kid floating next to me.

I shook myself awake. I was gasping to catch my breath. My flannel sleeping bag was damp with sweat and I felt tears leave my eyes. I composed myself there. Rick was sound asleep on the other side of the tent and couldn't offer much help. I shook my head, trying shake the feeling that had gripped me. I turned over and attempted to fall back into sleep.

Clairvoyant

Camp Life

Another day went by and I now relaxed on the wooden deck that the tent was set up on. The lawn chair in which I sat, overlooked the lake. The shimmering gold of the sun reflecting off the waves made for a tranquil evening. Rick was in the tent trying to hunt the wolf spiders that would appear every day, which was a typical pastime at camp. We kept the flaps tied open, so the tent was well lit and had some fresh air flowing through. I sipped on my canteen as I looked across to the other side of the Wisconsin lake. There were nice summer homes on that side, all of which had sleek motorboats docked on the shore. Made us a little jealous some nights when the bugs were bad.

From my right, I heard a thrashing in the woods between our site and the camp next to us. Down the hill, between the patch of thick trees that separated the two sites, came a line of scouts, marching like ants. The boys who came from the neighboring site had to be at most twelve years old. Being that my tent was the closest to the forests edge, they walked right in front of me. The patrol even carried their little banner, tied to their leader's pack.

"Hey," I hollered at them. "What are you guys doing here?" I jumped down from the platform, to their level.

"We're seeing where the dead kid was, back off!" The clear ringleader squared up to me. I had to look down some considerable ways to meet this kid's glaring eyes, barely peering out from under his Smokey Bear-style hat.

"Look, you guys shouldn't be over here if that's the reason you came. Why don't you go on back to your camp?" I chuckled at the boy, who looked like he still had some of his baby fat left on him. He pushed me or attempted to do so. He ended up staggering backwards as I stayed where I was. From his utility belt, he drew a hunting knife and held its tip against my sternum.

"I fucking do what I want," He threatened. I smiled, then proceeded to laugh at him.

"What are you, like five? Who taught you to swear?" I mocked.

"I'm fourteen, you prick!" His little face was burning.

"You hear that Rick? *Babyface,* here, knows how to swear!" He came from the tent with an arachnid skewered on his pocketknife.

"What did you call me...?" The fury in his voice could be heard through his crooked teeth.

"I believe the name was Babyface," Rick pitched in.

"That's what I thought I said," I clarified, smirking. From that moment on, the kid no longer had a real name, if he even had one before. "Babyface" was the only name he was ever recognized by

26

for the rest of camp and perhaps the rest of his life. He slowly took his knife off my chest. "Now, take your little posse out of our camp," Rick slipped away without detection.

"You were the one who found him, weren't you?" He looked up at me, pointing at me with his blade. "So, how'd you do it, how'd you kill him?"

"Are you serious? I didn't kill him."

"That's not what I heard. I heard you were the one who killed him, cut him up in pieces, and you just reported it, so you wouldn't get caught."

"What you heard was shit, now just go away," My hot-headed nature was starting to lose its patience with the child.

"No, I think I can go wherever I want," Babyface continued to wave his knife at my face.

"I didn't know they let five-year old's play with knives like that. In fact, I didn't think knives that size were even allowed in camp at all," I taunted him more.

"It's a good thing they're not!" A hoarse voice came from behind me. It was Babyface's scoutmaster, who was with Senior and Rick.

"Oh shit!" His gang scrambled into the forest where they came from, some of them tripping and fell back down the hill. Babyface quickly hid his knife back in its sheath. His face was no longer blushed with hate, but with embarrassment. His scoutmaster gripped him by the arm as he took Babyface back towards his camp. The old man's yelling could barely be understood, but one could tell he was mad, alright.

"Thanks for that," I hit Rick on the shoulder as he stood next to me.

"Did you antagonize him at all?" Senior asked sternly, knowing fair well our history of stirring trouble.

"Well, a little," I admitted.

"Ok," He sighed his tenseness out. "Well, try not to pick any more fights with, uh, *Babyface*," He shook his head as he walked back up to his tent. It was late now, but we stayed up simply to hear the kid get screamed at for sneaking in overly large knives to camp and for threatening other scouts. Rumor has it that he hid a machete in his sleeping bag and throwing knives in the fishing box. Eventually, later in the night we fell asleep.

Now, I don't know what it was that woke me, but I would soon come to regret it. My eyelids softly opened to meet the darkness. Even though the air was dark, I could sense that something was amidst. A blue silhouette on the black air.

"Rick," I hissed. "Junior!"

"What?" I heard him roll over from his sleeping bag. Only the name he hated most could wake his heavy sleeping.

"Shine your flashlight over here, I think there's something in my bug net," My body was still cocooned in my sleeping bag and only head was able to move around. He sighed with annoyance but went for his torch anyway. He clicked it and the beam of light brought forth the origin of the silhouette. A wolf spider the size of my hand, dangled on its string only inches off my face. I froze in terror. The beast of a spider knew it had all power over me and could do exactly what it wished. Unlike regular spiders who simply catch their prey in webs, wolf spiders aggressively hunt down their food with pure ferocity. The monstrous fiends were always on the prowl.

"Heh, you're fucked," He clicked his light off and rolled back to sleep. I stayed awake shivering in fear. I brought my trembling hands out from my bag and slowly lifted them to about where I remember the spider being. I took a deep breath and clapped my palms together. From outside my tent, painful screams could definitely be heard.

I met my boys at the breakfast table, in the dining hall. Babyface's troop sat next to the area we sat. So periodically, just to set him off, we would look over at his little gang and pretended like we were talking about them. We were, however, talking about our plan of action.

"So, I've asked some of the counselors if anything weird has happened here," Zeke started. "Apparently awhile back this one counselor got fired."

"No shit, people lose their jobs all the time," Allan snapped at him after staring at him blankly for a few, long seconds.

"No, no. That's not it. They say he went missing and no one's seen him since."

"I've also heard old man Neibel killed scouts and threw them into his lagoon," Jack added on.

"I'm being serious, that's what they said. And maybe he's still out there."

"I'm gonna have to agree with Jack and Allan here, Zeke. It sounds more like a ghost story," Joe concluded. Zeke looked to me to back him up. I shrugged as I held an icepack over the many fresh bites on my face.

"I heard they also caught a bigfoot in scoutcraft," Allan continued.

"You sure that wasn't your mom?" Jack snickered. Allan was quick to throw a sliver of toast at him, which triggered a hitting match between them.

We finished chowing down on our cereal and cleaned ourselves up for our morning courses. We had a little extra time beforehand, so Zeke and I hit up the trading post. In the afternoons, this place was popping, but mornings like this were always quiet at the little shop.

"Hey, Thor," Zeke and I waved as we walked in. All the scouts knew him by "Thor" because of his long blond dreadlocks and his enormous stature. Even if the scouts didn't know that was his nickname, it was instinctual to call him thus.

"How are you boys doin' today?" He asked as he leaned against the glass counter.

"Not too bad, just killing the time," Zeke pipped back. I went for the cooler to grab him and I some soda. I handed them to Thor as I pulled out my billfold.

"You're from the troop that found that kid, right?" The red 84 patch was sown on our uniforms.

"Yeah, that was us..." I replied.

"It's all a shame, he was young," I nodded, pressing my lips together. Thor could see the conversation made me uncomfortable. "Well, you guys have a good day."

I glanced over at Zeke as soon as we left the post.

"Wish people would stop asking, ya know? Seriously, why'd it have to be me?"

"If not you, it would have been the next passerby. This isn't a *you* thing, Lane, it just happened by chance."

"You think it was chance? You tend to be the one to believe in fate."

"I don't think he was there by accident, but this isn't God's way of making you suffer. You're letting this go to your head. Look we all saw the body, you just happened across him first. The world isn't singling you out," Zeke very rarely go heated over things, but he was quick to calm back down.

"I know, but it weighs on me. I can't sleep and when I do, I see him. I feel his conscious following me. I know it sounds crazy, but I feel responsible for finding him justice."

"And we will," Zeke took a sip from the bottle of pop. "You just need to keep your head."

We arrived in Scoutcraft on the moment that class was starting. On the way, we passed by signs for the "Eco Arena," which were posted all over campus. This arena was single handedly the most boyish thing that went down at camp.

Throughout the week, scouts would collect bugs and reptiles and bring them into the Ecology building. We caught snakes, turtles, frogs, salamanders, and big-ass spiders. Each year, there was a hunt for the illusive Rock-eating Recluse. The older scouts, namely Jack and Allan, would send the youngsters down into caves to try and catch this non-existent spider. Purely for sport and to pay retribution for being tricked into this when we were tenderfoots.

The arena happened when Ecology would get too full and needed to purge its space of more useless animals. So, the natural solution was to take different species and pin them up against each other in a big tank. After lunch, the boys and I decided to get in on some of the action and enter a competitor. Now, natural selection told us that the snakes would be the apex predator at camp and would always win the arena, but we liked to enter other creatures for the hell of it.

Traveling over to Ecology, we passed the boardwalk that crossed Lake Neibel. The "lake" was one of many lagoons in Camp Tomahawk, but definitely was the most infamous. The water was so green and murky, you could never see an inch into it. Yet the surface was always so still, as if a swamp thing was waiting below. Trunks and cattails stuck out from the marsh, creating enough shade to hide what was beneath.

It was rumored that there's a snapping turtle the size of a car the lurked in that bog, but no one ever had the balls to go looking for it. Most first year scouts were too scared to cross the causeway, and rather would take the long way to the Eco building. No one had ever even dipped their feet in the muddy water. Not until today.

We were on the far side of the lagoon, looking under logs for newts when we heard a rather higher pitch scream. We ran over to find that a little scout had tripped and fallen into the swamp. He landed on his back on an old stump, which the only thing between him and the demonic waters. He cried and thrashed his arms, kicking in the black water. The guys and I stood over him as he did so.

"Help me outta here!" He panicked as he splashed around.

"Oh shit, it's an alligator!" Allan pointed to the nothingness behind the kid. The youngin screamed even further. "It's a big one, too!"

"God! Help me already!" The kid's eyes were hidden behind tears of fright.

"Okay, okay, hold on," Rick groaned as he went to the woods near the lagoon. He dug out a long branch and hauled it over to the squealing scout. He reached it over to the kid. "Grab it!" His chubby fingers constricted the branch.

"Man, that gator is getting pretty close," Jack stirred the pot a bit.

"That's if the snakes don't get him first!" Allan kept on. Rick was nearly pulled in by the young scout who was further panicked.

"Watch it!" He barked at the kid. Eventually the scout pulled himself to his feet and crawled onto the boardwalk. His soaked clothes rained down and damped the wooden surface. Life was once again in his own hands. "You gonna be alright?" Before the kid could answer, Allan decided to give the poor kid one more scare.

"Are those leeches on your back?" The poor scream could still be heard as the kid ran over the hill into camp. At first, I was a little upset that Allan and Jack had kept terrorizing the boy, but before long we were all laughing unconditionally. I couldn't even be mad anymore.

As the lot of us stumbled into Eco, we caught up with one of our own first year scouts. He stood puzzled as he held out his sweaty palm. For in it, was a certain lizard-like creature.

"Whatcha got there?" I asked Riley, who I recognized to be the young scout that had witnessed Jay's body being taken away.

"I don't know... The thing is, the guys at Eco didn't know either," At second glace I noticed that this thing was unlike any other. We had been chasing newts and salamanders at camp for years, yet never had we seen a fiend of this sort. It was slimy and had a longer snout. Darken emerald scales lined its back. "I saw it crawl out of the swamp. Maybe the water mutated it, whatever it is."

"Huh," I puzzled. "Maybe."

We rolled up to the Ecology building. The fight club had already been established and no doubt the scouts were making bets on which snake would come out on top. Fangs lashed out as frogs leapt hopelessly away from them. The whole crowd would cringe with excitement every time an amphibian became dinner. We roared at the scene. It was a good thing moms never came into camp, cause this inhumane tradition of ours would surely be extinguished.

Riley dropped the abomination of nature into the arena. At first, it simply squatted there, bugged eyed amidst the bloodshed of its fellow four-legged. Rivaling gardener snakes picked up the new scent. Tracking along the grass, they nearly swam up to the creature. The serpent sprang out at it, but the abomination was quick to evade. They danced around, and we all stared in confusion as the creature simply avoided all of the snakes' attacks.

"Kill em already!" One overly scrawny boy with telescopes as glasses shouted from behind us. It was almost toying with the snake, who was getting tired of chasing the thing around. Eventually, it gave up and turned to the easier prey to feed on. Fleeing from the scene, the abomination scurried up and out of the cage and before we could catch it, it vanished into the sticks. We were awe struck at the very scene.

After the area wrapped up, we decided to stay back and talk to the guys at Eco about the rumored missing counselor. Mainly because Zeke insisted.

"Arron!" One of the Eco staff, who was cleaning up, came over to join our huddle.

"Yeah, Zeke?"

"We were-"

"He was, not we," Jack interrupted.

"Anyway, we were wondering about that staff member a few years back who got that one kid sent to the hospital?"

"What about him?"

"What happened to him? I heard he went missing," Arron sighed, then nodded.

"Boone," Arron started. "That's what we all called him. Benjamin Taylor was his real name," His voice was shaky, and we could tell that Arron was uncomfortable talking about it. "Yeah, he was the ideal scout. I mean, that's all he did was scouting and he knew his shit. He was teaching a younger boy to carve wood; the kid was being an idiot and was cutting toward himself and sure enough ends up slicing his hand open. We all knew Boone didn't do anything wrong, that it was the kid's own fault, but his father was a lawyer. So, a few stiches later, he had enough firepower to get Boone kicked out. He was so broken; I mean this was all he had. He had already aged out of his troop, so now that he wasn't allowed to work, he had nothing."

"But he isn't actually missing, right?" Allan nudged him on. Arron shook his head.

"I went back to his cabin to check on him and the place was all torn up and he was gone. No one had seen him since, not his family, no one in town. I've had my theories, but I doubt-"

"Doubt what?" I persisted.

"That maybe he's still in camp, somewhere. He knew how to survive; I wouldn't think he'd be crazy enough to do it though. I'm sorry, I knew him back then, it's hard to really talk about."

"I'm sorry, we understand," I apologized to him; whose eyes had allowed a few tears to drop.

"I know why you're asking," He looked dead at me. "The staff know about what happened when you got here. You're looking someone who did that, right? You're trying to find out who killed him?" He asked sternly.

"Yeah. That's what we're up to," I confirmed his accusation.

"I wouldn't dare go looking for him, in case of what I may find, but I'll help you. If he really is in camp, I think I know where he went. Before this Eco building was put up here, there was another. The trail is blocked off, but it should still be manageable. This, uh, 'Old Eco' is a bit of a hike out, but the trail eventually leads to the Outpost. No one has been allowed there for over a decade, my bet is that he's there. I don't think he's a murderer, but after this long alone in the wilderness, who knows. Just be careful," He turned away from us and went back to his task.

The crew meandered out of Ecology, though I intentionally fell back. As much as I liked being in the circle, I also found comfort in walking alone, able to clear my head of any angry thoughts. My hunch that the killer was still around was true. My vocation became my obsession, now I needed to find answers. I wish I wasn't so damn called to this, though. I wanted to drop it, I wanted to forget Jay's face, and enjoy my summer camp. But I couldn't; I was overwhelmed by the weight of the situation and how compelled I was to continue on for the boy's sake.

Eventually, I let my thoughts fade out. The natural sounds of the woodland seemed to come together in a symphony. The branches would creek and call with the wind. Birds chattered and harmonized with one another. Almost like a hundred languages all being spoken, yet all in perfect understanding of each other. Further into the nights, crickets would join in and keep tempo.

There was a presence then, of a mundane and earthly spirit. Sometimes she could just be felt, as if it was her way of saying, "this is how life was meant to be, life was meant to stay in the garden."

Most people are caught up in their own heads too much to notice her faint calling. That's why this camp was an oasis to so many scouts. For a short while, we could be away from the cities and civilization, and take in all this spirit had to offer. Even some of the guys I've meet who didn't believe in a god, felt this spiritual connection to nature.

"You think I wouldn't notice you wandered off?" My moment of tranquility was shattered when Zeke had ambushed me from one of the platforms in scoutcraft. "Someone needs to keep watch on you."

"Just thought I'd clear my head with some silence."

"Do you think he's telling the truth?" Zeke looked back toward Ecology.

"Sounds like it. It's all so crazy, this whole mess we're in."

"That's one way to say it. You always looked for adventure though, now you have one."

"No, this isn't an adventure. When we crawled through the sewers back home, or ran along the railroad tracks, I was content with that. Someone died, Zeke, this isn't some adventure of ours. This feels like judgment; retribution on our home turf. This is scary. I genuinely don't want to see how this is going to end. We have no idea what we're doing, no idea where this is going to take us. We're not as clairvoyant as we like to think."

"You really want to give up on this? This is the only real lead we've gotten and if we solve this, we could bring it into the cops and then we can get some justice for all this," Him and I started walking slowly back to our camp. We were the only two on the path. He knew I agreed with him. "I was thinking, tomorrow is Outpost day, so everyone will be hiking there. Arron said this trail to Old Eco continues on to the Outpost. We could take that trail and just check it out. We hike faster than the younger kids anyway, if we leave early, we would have enough time to really search the place and still get to the Outpost the same time the others do."

"That's not a bad idea. You think we'll find anything?"

"Yeah, it makes sense. Do you?"

"I kind of hope we don't find anything, maybe what we need is for the trail to go cold," I shook my head. "Maybe then we move on with our lives."

We wandered on the now lonely trail. The evening sun provided golden rays through the dusty overgrown forest.

"It does feel like judgement, though" Zeke eventually agreed. "Years of living freely has finally caught up. Whatever past evil went unnoticed here, it's now being paid for."

The One in The Woods

Mist radiated along the forest floor. Olden trees creeped through the ghostly aura and reached their branches across the sky. For all I knew, I was alone as I walked down the quiet rut. From the fog, a bear appeared to me. The grizzly was still hazy as it grew closer. Green leaves parted as its soft, but powerful steps brushed past. Its fur glistened in the rays that caught the misty forest. The bear presented itself to me, coming not an arms-length away. There was a moment of perfect serenity.

A shrill of a loon came from behind me. I turned as it's scream sent shivers down my back. The bird cast a shadow over the trees. It studied me intently with its blood-red eyes. I turned away from it, to find the bear had collapsed and turned to bones. Its bleached skull rested at my feet.

I took off running, disoriented as I did so. Not only was I unaware of my direction, my sense of up and down blurred together. The black bird flew after me, bringing a blanket of shadows with him. This vertigo slowed me down and nauseated me further. I felt my feet stager as they fell from beneath me. Darkness rolled into the woody night, a darkness that overtook me.

I felt myself seize as I woke up, struggling to catch my breath. My tired eyes let streams of tears fall as I sat up. I scooped my ragged shirt up off the floor where I left it last night and used it to wipe my face of sweat and tears. After sitting up and taking some deep breaths, I walked out of the tent, the early sun warmed my back and just nearly lit up the lake's glass surface. The deep sigh I let out was the only sound that moment. Mist rose from the lake like specters and swayed in the dawn's breeze. I threw on my shirt, went back in the tent, and shook Rick awake.

"It's about time," I said quietly.

Softly, I made my way to Jack and Allan's tent. They were more resilient to being woken up, but after I flipped Jack's cot over, they were more willing to comply. Zeke met us at the road. We made sure not to wake anyone else as we slipped away, the faint crunch from our hiking boots was all the noise we made. We were always good, as a crew, operating with discretion. Just as long as we weren't fighting and horsing around.

Zeke led the march, since he was the one who mapped out the entrance to the abandoned trailhead. The route took us to the beach, but quickly diverted into the woods. When the last of us walked into the narrow trail, we seem to disappear in the brush; away from the world of that which could be seen. Not too much further was the actual trailhead. A clearing just small enough for us all. The sign was overgrown with weeds and branches, but it clearly read, "Ecology."

"This is it," Zeke turned to us. "Lane, you wanna take it from here?"

I patted Zeke on the shoulder as I stepped passed him. One by one, we scaled over the rotted gate that forbid us from entering. The trail wasn't kept–no larger than a deer trail by now–yet I felt confident following it. Zeke followed me, Jack and Allan close behind, and Rick took up the rear. The woods went infinitely around us, which always brought forth an eerie presence. How we looked so desperately alone, yet we could have walked right by something and never noticed. Us lost boys could have been stalked and would have never known; no wonder pagans feared the forest so fiercely. This feeling never dissuaded any of us from spending long durations of time out here, but it was in the back of all of our minds.

"So, what's the contingency plan again?" Rick called ahead to me.

"Joe is hanging back to cover our tails. If anyone asks him where we are, he tells them that we had to run to the trading post and that we'd catch up later at the Outpost."

"Senior saw us, ya know?" Jack interjected.

"What?" I stopped and turned to Jack.

"When we were walking out of camp, he saw us."

"Fuck," Rick let out under his breath, as he was tying his neckerchief around his head like a bandana.

"If he wanted to, he would have stopped us. I think he knows what we're up to."

"Maybe," Zeke agreed with Jack.

"I guess whether we get in trouble or not, doesn't matter. We're still going to Old Eco, if there's a consequence it wouldn't affect the mission until after," I added. The others nodded in coalition. Our parade took off once again, making way toward that cabin deep in the woods.

"I mean, unless we got killed," Allan said to Jack, who hit him to be quiet. "That would affect us," He continued anyway. That topic was haunting all of us, I'd be lying if I said we weren't all a little scared of what we would stumble upon. Sure, we thought we were invincible, we were boys in our late teens, but we had our limits whether we knew them or not.

I don't know how the others coped with all of this, all the trauma. We were chasing ghosts. In my book, we were a fable. I didn't want to admit to myself that this plot was real. More comfortable, was I to think that this was some twisted story. We were the Fellowship of the Ring and this was our march into Mordor, like in some book. I hated thinking about it that way, it seemed naïve, but that innocent lie kept me going over the cold truth that someone had actually died. I couldn't bear the thought of evil existing outside the fable.

Old relatives of mine had passed away, but this was a kid who was murdered, this was different. I didn't know him, but I can relate to whoever is mourning for him. Back in 5th grade a classmate of ours died. Now I didn't know him that well, he wasn't a part of our company, but that's when I really figured out what it meant to die. Someone that I would normally pass in the hall or occasionally sit next to at lunch was just gone. There were those who counted the days since his death, marked the anniversaries, always posted a flyer. That wasn't me, even when my grandma and grandpa passed. The globe kept spinning. Something just didn't seem healthy to me about trying to stop the earth from turning each year, on the anniversary of one's death. Maybe I'm just too stoic. I guess, in the end, I'm just hoping this fable has a happy ending. Since right now, I was nearing a breaking point. I felt that tensions were rising with no hope of closure or resolution.

We could tell the lake wasn't far off from where the trail was. Loons shrieked, and their echoes rang throughout the otherwise quiet wilderness. Their shrill call made even grown men shiver.

"That oughta wake you up," Jack chuckled from the back. We came to a setting where the lake made an inlet. The trail ended at the shore and picked up across the way. Between the two shores was a bridge of sorts. Wooden pallets with barrels underneath them were strung together to make a floating walkway.

"Fuck this," I muttered as I tried to step on the first pallet. My weight pushed the pallet below the water. Our clique convened on the bank.

"We can't just go around; the woods are too thick here," Zeke pointed out.

"Yeah, we may just have to get our boots wet," Jack added on. I sighed, stepping out again on the pallet. It sunk into the marshy water. My balance was worse than I thought, but I was able to gain control and step onto the next one.

"Hurry up, Lane, I'm gonna miss my birthday!" Allan taunted me from behind.

"Piss off!" I laughed as I took another quivering step. The other, lighter, guys followed me with more success on the bridge. Not that I was fat, just more muscular than my skinnier friends. Now that all of us were on the bridge, each pallet tugged on each other, which made passing more difficult. I felt the one I was standing on jolt backwards.

"Dammit," Zeke let out, immediately after a splash. I peered over my shoulder to see Zeke yanking his foot out of the marsh. "I slipped," he muttered shamefully. It wasn't long after that we made it across.

We pressed further, even with the swamp water sloshing around in Zeke's boot. To keep myself more or less entertained, I started humming a tune familiar to the boys.

"One evening as the sun went down and the jungle fires were burning," Zeke caught on and I joined him in singing.

"Down the track came a hobo, hiking, and he said, 'boys I'm not turning,'" the others jumped into our ragtag choir.

"I'm heading for a land that's far way, beside the crystal fountains. So, come with me, we'll go and see The Big Rock Candy Mountains!" None of us were particularly good singers, but we weren't half bad either. We chanted the rest as we marched up the further into the deep. The ferns grew thick in this stretch. They protruded from the delicate red dirt.

I usually hiked with my head down, looking precisely where I placed my feet. I stopped myself just then. Where I had almost laid down my boot, was a metal ring of teeth that barely poked out of the leaves. I froze, and my hands began to shake. The others soon came to me to see what I was shocked up over.

"Shit," Rick let out. He took his walking stick, that he had only recently picked up and lightly set it down in the center of the ring. The jaws snapped shut with such fury, they busted the stick in half. "A fucking bear trap!" We had seen them before; poachers hid those death snares in our local camp. Nearly stepping on one, though, was terrifying.

"Guys, I think we're here," Jack pointed out and we all looked up in unison. Behind the bend, through the branches we could see the makings of a building.

"I guess, just watch your step," I started forward. We were slow to approach the cabin, staying low as we crept. The cabin was built Lincoln Log style, but age had not been kind to it. Moss grew thick on the walls and vines hung dying from the roof. A crude wind chime was also suspended on the patio. Its unwelcoming song rang throughout the perimeter. The scenery was dead as a whole.

On my lonesome, I snuck to the entryway. The wooden boards creaked as my weight pressed down on them. I worried that whoever might be inside could have heard, but there was nothing. I continued forward, peering through the screen door. Turning back toward the guys, they nodded in assurance for me to continue. My breath was shaky as I pulled the door open.

"Jesus," I whispered. The place was trashed and smelt absolutely horrid. Berries and other edible plants were overgrown in their pots and spilled out onto the tables they rested on. The others came in behind me after seeing it was safe to come inside. I made my way over to a bunk that had a compilation of cut-up blankets and animal skins.

"Check this out," Zeke called to us. In the corner where he stood, a tape recorder was set up next to an amateur radio.

"The hell are these?" Jack picked one up.

"They're recordings," I also grabbed one. "Here, put one in," I handed Zeke one of the multitudes of cassettes. He slid the dusty tape into the recorder. It took some time to get everything fired up, hearing only static at first. I imagine it was powered by the windmill that was tied to the side of the building. Just then his voice filled the terrored silence.

"Holy shit!" Zeke shook.

"Food's been scarce," The man coughed as he began his dialogue. "I've trapped a couple of rodents, but nothing to hold me over long. I, uh, I had to make a run to the camp, they didn't see me, but I just had to see how things were going. It's been too long... The plants aren't bearing much fruit now that it's getting colder. I'll have to stock up on pine branches before winter. Pine tea ain't the greatest, but, um, it's better than hot water. Anyway, Boone out," The clip turned to static. We all sat there; mouths wide open. I turned away from the machine as Zeke shut it down.

"Uh, guys..." Allan nudged Jack, without moving his eyes. Not far from us was an ungodly blood stain on the floor. Rags were soaking up most of it.

"Jesus Christ," Rick gasped. Flies buzzed around the pool. "I think we've seen enough."

"Agreed," I muttered. We filed out of the Old Ecology building, leaving no trace of our presence. The trail picked up on the opposite side of where we had entered the clearing. Rick and I were in the back, chatting. "You think he did it?"

"I mean, it would add up, but we have nothing if you think about it. Yeah, we confirmed that this guy isn't just a local legend, but we can't say he was a part of it. There's no evidence."

"I just get uneasy thinking about it. It's just surreal that this is even happening, you know? This is-" A branch snapped nearby. Rick and I bolted back behind the cabin, while the other three up ahead took cover in the brush.

Rick peered around the corner toward where we heard the snap.

"Shit," He spun back around. "It's him," I could see the guys in the trees from my angle, but they couldn't see Boone approaching. We heard the cracks on the patio as well as the door opening.

I glanced back to Zeke and the others and mouthed "run." They didn't comprehend so I tried again to relay the message, pointing back to the trail. They crawled back to the path then took off running. From inside, I heard the man shuffle around. There was some clanking of pots and I could make out that he was rummaging through his stuff. There was a window above where we were kneeling, Rick dared to peek over the ledge.

"Get down," I hissed at him. He waved me off with his hand. Rick studied him through the pane.

"He knows someone's been here," Rick turned to me. "He took the cassette out of the recorder."

"We need to go," I ordered sternly.

"Fuck," Rick dropped down. "He saw me!" I muttered some curse words of my own under my breath. "Alright, we're running," We bolted from the cabin toward the trail. The only sound I could hear over my heartbeat was the slamming of the screen door followed by several gunshots.

"Dammit!" I gave in and turned back to see him. His mane veiled his piercing bronze eyes. His clothes were ripped and torn. His body was lean and rough. His face was scarred and unkept. A few more rounds went off as we escaped into the forest.

We ran with all the haste our legs would allow. Our feet kicked up the earth and beat up the trail. The ground quaked as we ran. I was the only one of the guys not on the cross-country team, but I kept up now. I can't say how far we ran; I could barely see anything. Zeke physically stopped me, bringing us both to the ground. I got up from the dirt and was bent over, gasping for air.

"What the hell was that?" Jack asked. I looked up at him, still catching my breath.

"It was him," Rick gasped. "We saw him."

"He shot at us; I don't know how we're not dead!" I pitched in, wiping the sweat off my brow. Zeke put his hand on my shoulder, comforting me. I propped myself up, finally stabilizing my breathing. "We should get to the Outpost," I started off, diverting subjects. The others looked at one another then were soon to follow behind.

Our company was short to reach the road, we hurdled the barrier that had kept scouts out of that head of the trail. The road was the usual pathway to the Outpost, so now we were officially on track. Our troop traditionally walked the few miles, but other, less ambitious, troops took the shuttle known as the "Cool Bus." It was a recycled school bus with the S and the H chipped off. Kids usually stuck their tongues out at us as they drove by, but those happened to be the kids who would get their asses handed to them in every camp game.

The Outpost was an old logging camp or, so it was made out to be. Workers there dressed in old-timey clothing and talked with a thick accent. There was a blacksmith there and a few other buildings to house staff and equipment. They had lumberjack challenges set up, like wood chopping, tree climbing, and log rolling. Livestock also roamed the dirt streets of the mock town. Chickens and goats wandered aimlessly around; none had ever run off despite there being no fence. But by far the best attraction at the Outpost was the brewery. Home brewed root beer that tasted like absolute heaven was their only good for sale, yet it was the only good that we needed.

We arrived there just before our troop. I had seen them from over my shoulder as the guys and I drew water from the well. I approached Joe, who was with the other scouts, and took him aside. I looked around me before starting, making sure no prying eyes were present.

"We found him," I whispered to Joe.

"Wait what?"

"He was there, Joe. The guy Arron told us about, Boone," I turned to face him directly. "He had to have been living there for years, he definitely went crazy."

"You saw him?!"

"Yeah, he shot at us. We're lucky no one got hurt. He had bear traps set up everywhere, too."

"Dang..." Joe sighed, then fixed his glasses. "Did you get any evidence, though?"

"No. We couldn't find anything to prove it was him," We started walking toward the other guys. They were perched on the side of the hill that overlooked the settlement.

"So, technically you guys didn't get any closer?" Joe prodded. "I had to cover for you and everything," He groaned.

"And we appreciate that, but this could still be a lead," Rick interrupted.

Joe and I sat down with the rest. Calm breezes and the ambient sounds of the Outpost provided a moment of relief for us.

"We're going to have to go back, you guys know," I openly stated.

"We can't now, he's probably waiting there to kill us," Jack replied.

"Maybe use us for stew. Cook us with some rabbits," Allan, right on cue, escalated Jack's comment.

"No, not now. I don't know when, but sometime. There has to be something there," I persisted. I needed there to be something. If this man was real, he better be the one we're looking for. I couldn't stand the thought of a second monster within these woods.

"Let's just enjoy being alive before we delve back in there, okay?" Chuckled Zeke. He was right though; I needed some respite from all that had happened.

"Well, I'm gonna get a beer to take off some of this edge!" I proclaimed as I stood and went for the brewery.

"Ah, hell!" Rick followed. Soon the others joined, too.

Enouement

It was the last full day of camp and we had our final test in Wilderness Survival. Essentially, we had to survive in the wilderness. It was a fairly straight forward task.

"We need more," I turned to Zeke, who had been right on my tail. We filled the middle of the pack that was being led into the deep woods.

"What do you mean?"

"I mean we need more to go off of, we need something tangible, some sort of evidence."

"Yeah, I agree, but how?"

"That's what I'm getting to. You see," I looked over my shoulder to make sure we were a safe distance from any of the other scouts on the hike, namely Babyface, whom I only recently noticed was in our class. "I asked where we were hiking out to, and it's right next to town. Which is where Jay and his Aunt lived," I handed Zeke a map of Camp Tomahawk, with the region we were hiking to circled in red ink.

"You seriously want to sneak out of merit badge again?" Our badge leaders didn't think too highly of us slipping out of class all week to check up on rumors and search for clues.

"Yes. We could find out where she lives, ask her some questions," I heard Zeke sigh from beside me, where he now kept pace.

"What makes you think she'll want to talk about it so soon?"

"If I tell her that I was the guy who found her nephew, I'm sure she'll be sympathetic."

"So, what's the plan of escape?" He scratched his head, giving into the idea of leaving.

"The counselor doesn't stay with us. Once we get to the site, he'll be picked up. That's when we make our getaway. The others will be too busy building their shelters to even notice."

"It doesn't look like town is very far either, we'd still have plenty of daylight," He folded the map and handed it back to me, and I stashed it in my shirt pocket.

It dawned on me then, as if I was washed over with a sort of melancholy feeling, that this was my last week of camp ever. I would never be walking these trails again. Never get to make these memories with my brothers again. It slipped by me; I didn't even think to grasp it. A couple hundred bucks to be here and I missed it. I missed out on the heart of camp because I was so damn obsessed with trying to solve this case. As if I slept the whole week. I let it weigh me down and I dragged my friends with me. That was it, a day more and that's the end of scouts for me. I had already earned my Eagle rank, so did the rest of the guys. There was nothing left to offer us anymore. I could have stayed back, the times I snuck away. I could've stayed and taught the younger boys a thing or two about life, the way all the men before me had done when I was younger. But hell, I'm too far gone. I've sacrificed too much to hang it up.

We walked a bit further, to some arbitrary spot in the woods, where woodpeckers were busy at work. Our counselor stopped there and waited for the rest of the parade to catch up.

"You guys are to camp here tonight!" He announced in a matter-of-fact way. "Make your shelters just how we learned in class, but only use dead material that you find. I don't want to see anyone cutting down trees. You might as well make a campfire, too. It'll get cold if your shelter isn't made correctly. Alright, I'm gonna take off. If you're still alive when I come back tomorrow, you pass," He turned and went further down the trail that we were previously on. Scouts immediately dispersed into the forest to gather dead branches. I had Zeke follow me as I walked in the direction that ran parallel with the trail. Keeping far enough back so the counselor couldn't hear us trampling along.

"Hey Lane," I turned my head to Zeke. "Can I tell you something?"

"What's up?"

"Okay, I haven't told anyone this, so you can't tell the guys."

"Okay," I chuckled

"I maybe, sort of, kind of like Anna."

"Andersen?" I asked.

"Yeah, she's on the cross-country team with me. But you can't tell her or anyone!"

"I won't, I promise," I continued to laugh.

"What?" He hit my arm in irritation.

"Nothing, you just made it seem like you were going to come out of the closet or something. I won't tell anyone about your crush."

"Good, cause I'm pretty sure she likes Allan."

"Really? I don't know what they see in him, but I know a *lot* of girls who like him."

"I know! What the heck?" We went on further. "So, what about you, who do you like?"

"Nope."

"What do you mean, 'no'?" I stopped and faced Zeke.

"You cannot, by any means under the sun, tell anyone," I pointed intently at him. He threw his hands up. I sighed, ran my hands through my blonde hair in contemplation. "I like Emily," Zeke's face light up with laughter.

"Emily, as in Rick's sister Emily?" I turned away in disbelief that I let that secret out. Zeke still stood shocked as I continued to walk away.

"You can't tell him!" I called back. He ran to catch up.

"Dude imagine having Senior as a father-in-law," I shook my head. "I can see it now, Uncle Rick and Papa Lane. Out back, having a few beers as Emily plays with the kids," He sighed with contentment. I shoved him over into the sticks. He staggered up and not long after we came to the road.

"Shit, get down," We dove into the ditch. Our counselor was standing where the trail met with the dirt backroad. A truck was barreling toward us from our right. Its tires threw up dust as it came to an abrupt stop. Our counselor hopped in the tail.

"They won't last an hour," he laughed with the other camp staff in the truck. It whipped back around and charged back to where it came. After the dust settled, Zeke and I crawled out of the ditch. We both instinctually turned to the left, being that the truck came from the other direction; from camp.

The road was never-ending and most lonesome. An occasional crow was the only company we got on our hike. Zeke and I walked side by side along this trail, not saying much as we went. Forests halted where a field took over. It stretched out on both sides of the road. Hay bales were scattered about it. On the horizon, a church came into view.

"Maybe we can check that out," Zeke pointed out to me.

"Yeah, if anyone's home, they'd probably know her. The town's pretty small."

"My thoughts exactly," He nodded his head. His curls we rougher looking now, it was easy to tell he'd been trucking though the woods. Bits of leaves had nestled their way into his mangled, bushy hair.

We drew nearer to the building. It was old and crooked looking. Paint was chipping off of the once white panels, what was left had faded to grey. "Long Lake Church," the post read, as we approached the concrete steps leading up to the entrance.

We each opened one of the double doors. The inside was stuffy. A faint, almost ethereal light beamed from the panes of intricate stained glass. Two shallow rows of pews lined the interior, with a carpet leading up to the altar. At this altar, was a man who had been praying. He stood but kept his gaze on the cross that was bolted into the front wall.

"Why have you come here? Worship isn't until Sunday. What do you want?" He turned fiercely; his eyes bloodshot as though he had been crying for some time.

"Nothing, we were-"

"Looking for someone in town, we figured you would know them," I interrupted Zeke, who was attempting to leave.

"I can't give away any information about the congregation. I'm sure you understand."

"I see, thank you anyway," Zeke went for the door. I grabbed his bicep and pulled him back.

"We're looking for Darlene Edgar," I proceeded. "We're friends of her nephew. We've been going through a hard time lately, with his passing and all. We wanted to pay our respects to her personally, since there wasn't a public funeral."

"So, it has to be," He sighed. "It would seem that she needs some faith, too," The pastor went into the office and took to the church registry to find Darlene's information. "He was the only family she had left, they've had a lot of misfortune, the Edgars. His parents died when Jay was quite young. I hope you find her," He tapped his finger on the address. "Godspeed, gentlemen."

"Dude, we shouldn't have lied to the poor guy," Zeke turned to me when we left the sanctuary.

"But we got what we're looking for, did we not?"

"I mean, I guess. It just feels wrong. We are seriously stepping over the line just to get some peace of mind."

"I want to think it's more than that. We're getting justice for someone who was murdered. I just can't think of not going through with this. I need to find out for him. Jay deserves to know."

"As long as this crusade is for Jay and not you," Zeke swallowed.

We continued onward down the dirt road. Intersections were few and far between. Holy Island Road was what crossed our path. The road wasn't a terribly long. It was shaded by trees that tucked old buildings away, holding them against the shore. There we found Darlene's house.

"This is it," Zeke muttered as we came to an old mailbox that read "Edgar," though it was hardly legible. It was a fading and exhausted house, seeming to be in its last years. We proceeded up to the door. The porch was covered in dust and the doorknob was broke. I gulped down my nervousness and turned to Zeke who nodded at me to continue. I knocked lightly on the door frame, being that the screen door was too weak to have been knocked on. There was no answer. I tapped on the frame once more.

"Yes?" Echoed faintly from within.

"Miss Edgar?" A figure came from the shade of the indoors. She was thin and short. "My name is Lane, this is Ezekiel," I gestured to my friend next to me. "Uh, do you have a moment?" She brought us into her home. It was dim and dusty; the widows hid behind the thick shades. She sat us at her kitchen table, which was covered in newspapers and an ashtray. "We're here to talk about your nephew, um, I know that's probably hard for you," She nodded and looked off from us.

"My boy was buried yesterday. It's a sham, the whole bit," She stern gaze came back to us. "An 'enouement' is probably the best word for what I'm feeling."

"A what?" I seeked for some clarification.

"Enouement. It's coming to the future and realizing it is not at all how you wanted it to be. My past self would be disappointed to see where this life landed."

"We understand," Zeke spoke softly for us.

"Why would you say it was sham? His funeral," I persisted.

"Well, the police said it was an accident, that he drowned," She shook her head. "Jay didn't like the water; he would never have been out there."

"He was wearing clothes too, wasn't he? When they found him, he was in street clothes, right?"

"Y-yes. How did you kn- who are you?" She became visibly uncomfortable.

"Miss Edgar, I found Jay. I found him in our camp Sunday morning," Her eyes of unsettledness turned to a deeper mood. One of sorrow and weight.

"I am sorry. On no one, I wish to have to see what you saw. An open casket is one thing, the setting cushions the blow, but another is to see someone like that when you don't expect it," She got up and went to her bookshelf. "Hmm, enouement," she whispered to herself. She pulled out a notebook from her collection. Skimming the pages until she had reached her desired place. She reminisced on whatever was on the page. Her soft smile faded into a deep depression.

"You know as well as us that something much darker happened," I looked up at her. She abruptly put her book back where it laid.

"He usually went off in the woods on his own. I guess it's my fault that I filled his heart with quotes and poems of adventure. He was missing the night before, I didn't pay it mind, I had thought he went to a friend's place. He was always independent, you see."

"Did he ever wander into the scout camp?"

"It's possible, I didn't bother ask ever where he went. I knew he never went anywhere particular, just that he *went*. I wanted to give him the privacy of keeping his adventures close to himself. You guys surely understand that wanderlust, I assume."

"Yeah," Zeke chuckled. "We like to trample around the woods back home."

"Then you're lucky you didn't meet the same fate Jay did," Darlene sighed. "We all know that his death was not an accident, whatever I can do to aid you to some answers, I'd be willing to help. I also need some closure."

"I guess we just wanted to know what you knew. And to see how you're holding up," I began. "We might have a lead, but only hunches. Nothing substantial. There's an abandoned cabin that's in a remote region of camp. Rumors said that someone was living in it, so us and the other boys went to check it out..." I paused. Not sure where to spare the details to her.

"Turns out those rumors were true. We didn't find anything that confirmed Jay was ever there. But we saw the guy who's been living out of it. So, we think he may be involved in this somehow, but we didn't have enough time," Zeke finished.

"We know this isn't settling news, Miss Edgar," I didn't know how to comfort people in these times. "I'm sorry if we brought you more pain."

"This is a lot to take in..." The old woman sat herself down. "The sheriff wouldn't hear me out. Wouldn't answer any questions."

"But why wouldn't they investigate at all? They just called it an accident before they even did the autopsy?" I filled my voice in frustration.

"I don't know," She said. I realized it was not my fight to get angry in. "May I ask something? Why is it that you involved yourselves in this?"

"I just feel," I had a hard time finding my words in the moment, but I talked slowly and quietly. "Burdened. I found him and I felt so drawn to Jay. It's hard to explain this connection I feel with him. I felt such a tender remorse, as if me finding him made me responsible. As if I needed to be the one to find justice for him. Darlene, I am so sorry for what you've had to go through," I stood up and wiped my eye. "We will do everything we can, for Jay."

On our return, not a lot of words were spoken. The sun was going down behind our backs. That conversation re-ignited my fire for the situation. Not only did I truly feel compelled to find justice, now I made a vow before his family to do so. I would have to push myself to the end, I would have to finish this.

We reached the trailhead at the peak of dark, it took a bit before we could see the faint luminosity of the fire the other scouts had set up. As we drew near, I saw the boys grab torches from the pyre, they waved them around in our direction.

"Wait, it's not a bear!" One of the younglings proclaimed. They stopped their charade with the torches, throwing them back in the fire pit.

"Where have you two been?" Babyface stepped forward.

"Making our shelters," I snapped back. Zeke remained quiet. He walked right up to me.

"You snuck off again, didn't you? You're always leaving, sneaking off. You probably killed someone else this time!" The other scouts began to snicker and jeer. "Unless you can show us your shelters, that's the only explanation! I wonder where we'll find the body this time," I turned and walked from the kid. Zeke followed. A rock hit the back of my head. I stopped dead in my stride. "Answer me!" I turned back, clenching my jaw. He pushed me past my breaking point. "Who else did you kill?"

I threw a hook and socked him right in the mouth. He fell and began to whimper after his injury.

"Not so tough are you!" I punched and beat him again.

"Lane, that's enough! He got what they deserved!" It was Zeke.

I kneeled next to the kid and gripped his hair, so he would be facing me. "Next time you pick a fight, pick more wisely," I left, fuming. The tension of the events finally broke. Violence was the only therapeutic release I ever seemed to get.

Morning came, and the sun provided enough light to replace what the fire had given us. Our counselor came back for us, despite what some were beginning to worry.

"Good morning, ladies, how-" he paused. He saw the bruises on Babyface. I hid my battered hand in my pocket. "What happened?!" No one spoke up. The counselor sighed and began to turn away.

"It was him!" Some dweeb pointed me out. I shot him down with my eyes.

"Yup," I muttered beneath my breath. "It was me."

"What the hell were you thinking?"

"We had a mild disagreement," I stated bluntly.

"Don't get smart with me, boy! When we get to camp, you're going to explain what happened to your scout master."

"You did what?" Richard Senior questioned back at the campground.

"I got in a fight," I was straightforward with the man. He scratched his head.

"I know this isn't you. Sure, you and the guys like to horse around, but I know you would never attack some other scout out of anger. Definitely not living the Scout Spirit, definitely not acting like a Patrol Leader," He shook his head. "We should have never stayed. We should have left that night. I know what it's done to our troop, specifically you. It's driven us mad. Everyone was so on edge, we even forgot to have our troop ceremony."

"We forgot Jolly Richard," I huffed.

"Do you know how much extra room that pirate costume took up in my tent?" We both chuckled to fill the painful moment. Each year we did this skit at our closing ceremony where Senior dressed up as the pirate, namely, Jolly Richard. It was a weird and outlandish charade like all the other skits, but we loved it. We quickly grew to a bitter kind of silence.

"I realized this was my last Tomahawk. I wasted it," I looked down at the table we had been sitting at.

"I don't blame you for it. Looking for answers," He sighed. I looked up at him.

"We didn't get anywhere though."

"Maybe not, but you guys knew it was right. You knew there was more to it then what the police report said. In fact, I would have been disappointed had you not gone after it," He took a sip of his coffee, then up and went without another word.

Clairvoyant

The Lost Tale

A month had passed since I came home from camp. With that, so passed the events that took place. They were no longer alive in my life. I still had the nightmares, but they grew easier to ignore. I spent the rest of that summer either sheltered in my room, or out trying get as far away from home as possible.

"I'm going out!" I would call to my parents as I was already out the door. The guys and I spent a lot of our time together, so my folks knew my general whereabouts. I would hop into my Cherokee and speed to their houses, all relatively close to each other. The route was always the same. First, I would swing by Rick's.

"I'm gonna hang out with the guys," He would announce as he came down the stairs.

"No, you're not," His mom was always a roadblock in our adventures. So as usual, Rick would go into the kitchen and argue with her. I waited in the entry way until they hashed things out. Rick's three younger siblings ran around the cluttered house, all screaming their lungs out. Emily came down the stairs to get them under control. Her dark hair was up in a messy bun.

"Oh hey," She mockingly greeted me. Then cracked a smile.

"Hi," I chuckled and scratched my head.

"Lane, I can't go unless I get the dishes done!" I glared back at my friend. Then, I proceeded into the kitchen to help the poor soul.

Next, we went to Jack's house. Rick and I came inside.

"Hey boys," His mother always greeted us warmly. Nolen, Jack's little brother, would toddle up to us and give us hugs.

"Hey there Nolen!" I ruffled his already messy hair. He was everyone's little brother. I spent plenty of Saturdays babysitting him and reading his favorite book, *Where the Wild Things Are.* It was charming that he could never remember how the story ended, which provided limitless entertainment. Jack descended from the upstairs, half changed and brushing his teeth. "You ready?"

"Wait, we're hanging out?" Rick and I looked at each other in annoyance. Even though we went through this charade almost daily, he never seemed prepared for our spontaneous adventures.

"We are now, let's go!"

We then bumbled to Zeke's house. We all filled into his unnecessarily messy house. Ezekiel's mom, as well as most of my friends' parents, helped out with our Boy Scout Troop.

"We're here to steal Zeke!" Jack proclaimed to his mother with gusto.

"Not until he finishes harp lessons. He has to play at church this weekend," She, for whatever reason, was stern in Zeke playing the harp. So, we all crammed on the couch, the little one that faced Zeke and his pitiful harp. All of us scowling at our friend, who was shaking with embarrassment. The only sound, other than the occasional sniffle, was the harmonic tunes of his instrument.

We sped off to Joe's, which was only a bit out of town. He lived on a little ranch, that owned a horse back in the day. His dad was in the yard practicing his archery. The older man, who was quiet and gentle as the breeze, was a deadeye with a bow. He waved as we went by.

"That man is a badass," Rick stated amongst us as we came to the door. We walked in his house and went immediately downstairs. As predicted, Joe was perched up on his couch coding a game that was hooked up to three box computer screens and a jungle of wires.

"Joe," No visible response. "Joe!"

"Huh?" He snapped out of the trance. "Oh, hey guys," He laughed at his own unawareness. He finished typing out his line of code, then ran out with us.

We took off from the dusty road that Joe lived on. The jeep kicked up rocks and formed a cloud of dirt behind us. We went back into the suburb which was nestled into the hill behind the lake city of Duluth. This was where our troop resided and where we all grew up. We were kings of this neighborhood, the closest thing to a gang our town ever saw.

Not far from the football stadium, was an abandoned soccer field. Cautious as I went, I drove beyond the stadium and across the way into this forgotten valley. It was overgrown and hidden behind the trees. We buried one of the soccer nets with branches and trees, making the perfect spot to hide a vehicle, which we often did. Not far from where we ditched the car, was a bridge that crossed over the railroad tracks.

The group of us went below to the tracks and followed them out of town. The line cut through the forest and went west all the way across the state. We hiked maybe a mile to where we would slip into the trees. For any observer, we would be lost from their view.

Within the thicket, we cleared out a camp some time ago. We would often come to this place, which we called Camelot. It was a place where we could truly be kings. Where we could return from the front lines of battle of our daily lives. We hung up our red patrol banner here when we weren't camping with the scouts.

Zeke and Jack went to work on the usual bonfire. They brought back downed branches and logs that the forest generously supplied us. Our hammocks were still strung up from the last time we visited. I reclined in mine, taking sips from my canteen, and taking in the fresh air.

"We could live out here!" I heard Zeke exclaim to himself.

"You say that all the time," Rick, who was already half asleep in his hammock, muttered out.

"I mean it, though," Zeke came more toward the camp. "We have a stream, plenty of wild berries, and we can the take taconite pellets on the tracks and smelt them down to make tools!"

"It wouldn't work, Zeke," Joe protested, tinkering with an old Swiss Army knife.

"And why not? No one would find us, we all have the survival skills for it," He paced excitedly.

"We have lives," I pitched in. "And families."

"So? We all have family issues. We could get away from that, get away from all the stuff in the world. If we lived in the wilderness, we could be free!"

"Have you ever read *Lord of the Flies*?" Joe countered.

"Uh, no."

"Well a group of boys surviving in the wild doesn't work. We'd kill each other."

"Just because a book says that'll happen, doesn't mean it will."

"Dude let it go, we're not living in the woods," Jack snapped.

"Whatever," He hung his head and went back to gathering kindling.

"I wouldn't kill you, Zeke," I attempted to lighten his spirits.

A train rumbled by. Its movement could be felt through the earth. Its boxes could be seen through slits in the trees. I stared off in its direction, mindlessly watching the cars go past. We didn't pay any mind to trains, as they came and went all the time. However, something appeared which caught me off guard. In the sliver of time between the cars, I saw the Boone. His dreads hung over his face, drenched in blood. He stood menacingly, like a wendigo, covered in the bones of his hunt. As quickly as he revealed himself to me, he was gone. I heard faintly the others in the background asking about Allan and how his time at band camp was going, but I was too engrossed by my vision. I got up from my hammock and slowly came toward the tracks. Right as the caboose rolled by, I proceeded to the other side, where I saw the man. My ears could faintly hear the others calling for me, but I didn't pay them any mind. The area was as it should be. No blood, no bones, and no Boone. I could feel someone walk up behind me, crunching on the taconite pellets as they walked the ditch.

"You alright?" I turned to Rick.

"Yeah, just thought I saw something," I said, not taking my eyes off the tree line.

Later in the evening, we went back along the tracks. The car was still exactly how we left it. In reverse order of how I picked the guys up, I dropped them back off at their houses. So, Rick was the last one to go.

"You still have those nightmares?" He asked me as he got out of the car. He went around and leaned up against my door.

"Oh, yeah," I nodded.

"The other night I had one," He proceeded to tell me. "I was back at that shack, the Old Eco building. I was dying. Bleeding out on the floor, all shot up. Boone was there, though I couldn't hardly see him, but I felt his presence. You know? I just knew he was there."

"Yeah, I gotcha."

"It was so long ago, but it feels like we were just there. Like only the other day we were getting shot at by that madman."

"I know what you mean," I sighed.

"Anyway, I should probably go. I'll catch you around."

I put the jeep in gear and rode on back home. The dull breeze blew my blonde hair back. My room was where I would immediately go when I got home. I found myself spending an unusual amount of time here; laying on my bed, tossing and catching my football. The weak green walls and the small floor were such a familiar sight by now.

My parents worried over me. To them, I only seemed to have life when I was running around with my gang. They weren't wrong. Though they would interrogate me, wondering why I wasn't happier. I usually locked myself in my room and left out the window when I couldn't stand them.

Only my thoughts would keep me company. My mind spoke ritualistically, chanting memories that did and didn't happen. Blurring the lines of reality for me. They forged details that I am unsure were present before. All these passing thoughts were from the events of camp. In particular, the one who lived in the woods. His image became increasingly distorted every time his face ran through my head. Like a werewolf, becoming increasingly monstrous.

Some days later, when I just needed an escape, I drove myself to the forgotten field and marched down the tracks to where I knew our secret camp to be.

"Needed to get out of the house?" I called to Zeke, whom I was not the slightest bit surprised to see.

"Yeah," He didn't turn from the fire he was tending.

"Parents fighting again?" I sat next to him.

"Heh, yeah," He chuckled and shagged his head. "I wish they would divorce already."

"Oh yeah?" I mumbled, thrown off by the statement.

"They hate each other. They actually yell out across the house 'I hate you.'"

"I'm sorry," I looked over to him. He just shook his head.

"They say they have to stay together because it's father's religious duty, but also for us kids. But you know, I would be happier if they got divorced."

"Hmm."

"It *would* be better."

"I don't doubt that, by the sounds of it."

"So, what about you? What brings you to Camelot?" He looked around him.

"Just my parents, they've been pissing me off lately," The fire's dance had my eyes fixed on it.

"Still scolding you to get happier?"

"Something like that. They think somethings wrong with me, like I'm depressed. Hell, even if I am, you can't just 'get happy,' you know?"

"Maybe it's not depression that's got you," I looked up at him. "I think we all lost a part of ourselves at camp."

"Maybe."

"Think about it, until we know what happened, like *really* know, it's gonna anchor us down. We're never gonna move on from it."

"Well what can we even do?"

"We could go back."

"Are you dense? We can't just go back to camp, we'll be seen and kicked out."

"What if we go after it closes for the summer?"

"Even if we did, what then? Where would we go?"

"We go back to Old Eco. We could visit Darlene again and see what she's found out," He got visibly excited.

"Hasn't she been through enough? We don't need to keep reminding her of what happened, she probably wants to move on."

"Then we just go back into camp. We can even stay in the tents, they're always there. This time, we'll be prepared."

"For what? Boone? He almost killed us last time. I don't want us to take that risk again!"

"I know you want to find out, I know you do!" He stood.

"Yes! I do," I got heated and threw down the rock I was fiddling with. "But not at the cost of our lives. We've asked enough of the guys; we can't ask them to do this again."

"They would in a heartbeat. We've always stuck up for each other. We've always been there when one of us needed. No matter what the cost was. Whether it was taking care of some bullies or even just doing chores to help each other out. You carried someone a mile when they were having a deathly allergic reaction. I know you're not scared of trespassing into the camp, we're trespassing now! We've gone through tunnels under the town, jumped over trains, broke into an abandoned asylum just because we wanted to. And when have we ever been caught?"

"Never," I rolled my eyes.

"Never! We were born to go on these adventures, live a little. Now *that* part of you was lost somewhere at camp. And I'll be damned if we don't get it back because that's who you are! You are our fearless leader. Where you go, we follow. But you're doing a shit job leading us right now," Over his shoulder, our red patrol banner was calling. Zeke turned to see what I was looking at. "That's who we are, Lane. We're warriors, taking action, charging in like flaming arrows! That spirit, that fire was lost somewhere in those woods. Now, you can continue to be like everyone else; sit inside, twiddling your thumbs, just waiting for something to happen. Or you can get your ass back out in the world and do something with your life!"

"Alright."

"Alright? Alright what?"

"Alright, we're gonna do this," He grabbed my arm, pulled me off of the ground, and gave me a bear hug.

"Hell, yeah we are," I said.

Zeke and I nearly ran out of the forest. We drove off to Jack's house and, more or less, kicked open the door.

"Jack!"

We then flew to Rick's.

"You guys can't come in," Emily's sass stood between us and the inside of the house.

"What? Why not?" Jack challenged, puffed up.

A faint "let them in" came from inside. Emily rolled her eyes at us as we blew into the house.

"Thanks," I said with a wink, as I walked past.

We gathered around the dining table, which was somewhere underneath the garbage and crayon drawings of Rick's younger siblings.

"...So, we go back to Tomahawk and find the rest of what we need to know," Zeke filled them in on the plan.

"But we would never be allowed to go, all of our parents would say no," Jack leaned forward.

"Here's what we were thinking," I began. "You guys tell your parents you're at my cabin for a few days. I tell my parents I'm at Zeke's cabin. My parents don't talk to any of your parents, so they can have a different story. And if everyone else's parents talk to each other, they'll all think the same thing."

"So, when do we go?" Rick asked.

"After camp ends for the summer. No one will be there, so we could move around freely," Zeke answered.

"Where are you guys going?" Rick's mom came from around the corner.

"The cities," Rick blurted out. "We were planning on driving down to the cities," She glared at me with her cold grey eyes.

"You're not driving anyone to the cities."

"I'm actually a good driver," I defended myself, laughing.

"You're not driving anyone to the cities," She took none of our jokes. She left the room, yet the decision we made was unchanged.

The Surreptitious Few

After what felt like an eternity, the time came. The time to return to the place that started this all. To the lion's den, where I knew he would be waiting. After churning the plan over in my mind for weeks, I was both extremely confident in our plan and most terrified. This paranoia lived in the traces of all my thoughts.

My parents were out of the house, doing errands that day. Old duffle bags were all packed with one vital exception. I proceeded down to the basement and opened one of our ancient closets. There inside, was my grandpa's hunting rifle. I stared at it for a moment, really contemplating whether or not this was something I was willing to do. I guess I would find out when the time came. The 'ot six made its way to the rest of my luggage as well as all the ammunition I found for it. I threw on my green and yellow letterman jacket and walked out the door.

I rolled up to Rick's house. He wasn't quite ready, but not long after I arrived, I left with him in the shotgun seat. His mom glared at us through the upper widow. We picked up Jack, who was actually ready this time, then swooped up to Zeke's. He was already waiting for us at the end of his driveway; backpack on and trucker cap over his pseudo-afro. He hopped in the rear with Jack.

We then finished our preparations by going to Joe's house, he wanted us to check in before we left. His road was scorched. The hot tires of the jeep disturbed whatever peace the road expected to receive that day. We pulled through his driveway as always. All us lost boys jumped out of our rickety ship. As we marched to the front door, the last member of our gang was waiting for our arrival.

"Hey guys!" He greeted us with a warm smile.

"Sup Joe?" The lot of us replied. Our line went downstairs to his lair. He handed us a bag full of junk food and soda. I was wondering if he would spare us his potato cannon, but it didn't seem to be in the grocery bag we were gifted.

"Remember, if any of their parents see you, say they're at my cabin. And if my parents see you, tell them I am at Zeke's cabin," I instructed him. He nodded. "I don't know how long we're gonna be gone, Joe," I paused. "Give us three days."

"Yes sir," He saluted. I gave him a hug and said farewell, as did the rest.

With that we were off, in a roar of dust and haste. The road took us eastward, into Wisconsin. Weather had been kind that day, the air was hot and dry, and not a cloud was in worrying distance of us. I drove particularly fast, as a hot shot teenage boy does.

The pines blurred together into a thick blanket of green. Where one branch ended, and another began, no one could tell. The wind blew our hair back as we sped along the forest highway with the windows down. The radio, I'm sure, was on and spitting out rockabilly music, but I couldn't hear it. Couldn't hear anything over the howl of the woods and the rumble of the motor. Though my eyes were fixed on the road, my mind couldn't help but to see the man who we were coming after. His ragged dreads, his torn clothes, his monstrous stance. If there was an evil that manifested into a single being, he was that being. He was the giant in my fable, the monster that all the villagers feared. And we were the poor souls the dukes of fate selected to take him out.

"So, what happens when we find Boone?" Jack asked from the rear.

"Check behind your seat," I quickly shot back. He looked and saw the telltale gun case sitting on top of my things. He turned back around and didn't say a word about it.

Along the way, the gas light came on. We pulled off at the next station we saw, being there weren't very many on the route. It was a desolate little place; I wouldn't be surprised if we had been their only customers that day. I filled the tank of the Cherokee and then our herd busted into the convenience store. I walked up to the teller to pay for my gas, the older lady asked where we were heading, and I tried my best to avoid an answer.

"Anyway, I'll just be paying for the gas," But while she was busy prying into where we were going, the guys behind me had grabbed every snack, candy, and soda can the store had to offer. They threw it all down on the counter in front of me. I then turned with an annoyed confusion and expected some sort of an explanation. "Don't we still have all the food Joe gave us?"

"Thank you!" Rick promptly chimed. The other two nodded with foolish grins on their faces, all of these met with a razor glare.

"And this stuff too," I shook my head.

We piled back into the vehicle and left that dingy place and took all of our shenanigans with us. The boys were gracious enough to get enough grub for even me to enjoy. Even though I hated them in that moment, I couldn't be too mad. We had this system, an unspoken way of life between us boys, that we all just spotted each other if we needed. Although, I bought half the store back there, last week Rick bought me lunch. Over time it evens out, so no one keeps track of who owes who, we just sort of pay for whoever needed it at that moment.

I could feel we were getting closer. The darkness was beckoning; it wasn't just my keen sense of direction though. There was an aura that loomed around the entirety of camp. Unseeable and yet it was noticed instantly. The weight of the task just now fell upon our shoulders. The laughter seemed to peter out and soon silence overtook the cab. As we crossed the threshold of the camp's borders, what was once home to us was now unfamiliar. For we knew better this time, this camp belonged to something else. It was never ours.

We broke the chain that held the gate in place and proceeded down the dirt roads. We drove the jeep all the way down to where we had camped only a few months ago. Dust and grime covered the bright red metal on the car. The old campsite beamed a homey feeling, the only welcoming sight we'd seen. A faded board that hung from the trees, read "Ironwood," the same campsite our troop has stayed in since the dawn of man. I suppose this gave us some sanctuary.

"You guys work on a fire, I'm gonna make rounds," I ordered as I went for the thirty ot six. I loaded five bullets into the rifle and then marched down the trail. It was still hot out; fall hadn't hit us yet with her colder weather.

The trail I proceeded down stretched toward the beach. Passed there, was the unmarked trailhead of the route that went to Old Eco. I slid my rifle under the wire fence and hopped the gate as I did, not terribly long ago. My boots started slow; my eyes scanned the bush as I went. There was no hunter in me, I didn't know how to track anything if I wanted to. I thought the task would be intuitive enough to just follow a set of footprints.

The ground was uneven and dry, not even deer tracks were found. My breath became heavy and filled with adrenaline. Dusk was creeping into place and perhaps the nightfall would bring Boone back to his hideaway. My feet carried farther than my heart would want. Yet my need to end this overcame the fear of all events. My legs proceeded deeper into the darkness, away from the rest of the guys, where I should not have gone. Before time grew long, I could see the illumination of the shack through the brush. Slower was my pace now, as I knew the bear traps were still scattered under fallen leaves. The shadows wove me seamlessly into the boscage, hidden from everything.

Old Eco stood hauntingly in the clearing of the forest. The last of summer's mist encompassing it all. Through the warped windows, I could see only a lone lantern. I could hear nothing over the backdrop of loons far off on the water. I waited; a long while I waited. My sweat chilled me to the bones in my body. Mosquitos sucked at my ankles and ate at my neck. The night air was getting cold, and I was growing tired of waiting. I lurched forward to the window. Peering in, I saw there was no one there. After quickly scanning my surroundings, I went into the cabin. Things were in the same mess as I remember them being. The recorder was already on though, I hit rewind and played the tape back.

"I, uh, know they've come looking for me," His quivering voice managed to say. "I heard them, as I hear all things. As I know all things," A deadly chill washed over me, to the extent where I was too frozen to turn off the machine. "I know why they want me... It's that boy, I had seen him before, but I never thought he would wander this far into camp. Look, um, if anyone should find this, consider this my confession. By the time anyone hears this, I will be far away from this place where no one could find me. My name is Ben Taylor. I have been living here, Tomahawk Reservation, for years in secret," He began to cry over the recording.

"I-I didn't mean to hurt anyone. Dammit! That's the same reason why I'm here in the first place! I just-just wanted to live here in peace. I love this camp so much. It's all I have! I, uh, set bear traps around this place to kill deer or other game. This kid, he stepped on one, but he was so far away from camp, no one heard him. I couldn't leave him to die. So, I got him free. He passed out and I tried to fix his leg, but it was broken so badly. I left him for a moment just t-to get some more firewood, but when I came back, he was gone. At first, I was scared that he would tell people where I was. Then I heard th-that he was found dead. I didn't mean for this to happen!" The audio ended, and the tape went to static. I immediately went for the recorder and ejected the cassette. I stowed it in my backpack and went for the door. Through the screen I saw the shadow of a tall, mangy figure. I threw open the door and lifted my rifle at him.

"You killed him!" I shouted at the specter. "You ran then, and you were gonna try to run now, you fucking coward!"

"I did," The voice echoed back.

"And I have your confession now!" It paused.

"I'm sorry! I am sorry for the pain I caused. Just let me live here, in seclusion from it all!"

"You killed someone," I shook my head. "You are going to jail!" The silhouette disappeared into the void. I fired off a round. Cocked the bolt and fired another. I ran to where I expected to find Boone's body, as the air was settling. There was nothing.

I took off after him. My legs ran faster and faster. My boots punished the dirt below me. Ferns slapped my jeans as leaves slapped my face. Like a wolf on his heels I hunted him, though I came to realization I was following no trace.

"Boone!" I hollered. "Boone!" I ran further into the twilight; the mist was clawing at my tired legs. I heard the snapping of branches like bones. He was near. I paced around, looking for where the footsteps where coming from. I slowed my steps, scanning as I went. The brush grew thick and twisted in on itself. Thrones and needles pierced my clothes and cut my skin. Only now in my anger did I realize he led me into this part of the forest, to slow me down. He knew this land better than I could ever hope to. No doubt he slipped away undetected by now, camouflaging with the vines and crooked trees. I yelled in frustration.

"Lane!" To my left, the guys stood in the distance. "Where the hell have you been?" I looked frantically about, scoping out the dead forest. He was gone. I trudged through the thicket to the trail the guys were on. Rick grabbed my shoulder firm and turned me around to meet him. "Where've you been?"

"Did you see anyone come through here?" I ignored their question. They shook their heads. "Dammit!" I kicked at the cursed ground.

"What the hell were you thinking?" Rick shoved me. "You just went after him and didn't tell any of us?" I didn't respond. He pushed me again. "And I suppose you didn't catch him."

"I did get something though," I reached into my bag and pulled out the tape. "He made a confession and explained what happened. He knew were here. He knew we were coming, but he doesn't intend on being caught."

"We can turn it in to the police and then it'll be over. They'd snuff him out and our part will be done," Zeke suggested. "We can be done."

"Yeah, but who knows how far he's gone now?" Rick had a point. He was quick to evade me; he would be difficult to catch.

"If we give this to the police, they'd have enough incentive to find him," Jack added.

"We're gonna find him. Between the police and us, we'll catch 'em for sure," I spurred on.

"Lane, once we turn in the tape, we're done. I don't know how much longer we should risk it," Zeke seemed eager now to get this all over with.

We made our way back to camp. Hiking in the dark was haunting. With a killer on the loose and everything. The moonglade glistened on the ripples of the lake. Loons still cried to one another, so did the frogs. Smoldering branches were in the place of where the guys left a fire earlier this evening. The tent was already set up and cleared of spiders. We had four cots in the tent, which took up all the floor space, so we left our packs outside as we crawled in. We laid in utter silence for a while, fighting the brisk, chill air.

"He said he knew everything," I muttered.

"What?" Jack asked.

"In the recording, he said he hears and knows everything in camp."

"That's literally impossible," Rick chipped in.

"I mean, he knew Jay had died after he got out of the trap. He knew we were coming."

"Do you think he knows where we are now?" Zeke asked, shaking.

"I don't know," Before any of us could realize how terrified we were, we were taken by sleep.

A beam of sun lit up the dusty tent the next morning. There was, however, another presence about.

"Fuck," Jack whispered as he sat up from his cot. "Fuck" was right because I saw it too. Just on the other side of the thin canvas tent was a huge mass. Jack was quick to quietly wake the others. "There's a black bear."

Of course, we left our bags outside, with all of our snacks in them. The bear was lethargic as it nosed through our stuff. I reached under my rack to where I knew I left the rifle. Pulled back the bolt, so I could see there was still a round in the chamber.

"We should sneak out the back," Rick suggested. We nodded. He untied the flaps in the rear of the tent, and we climbed up and over the railing. "We should be able to scare it off now, I just didn't like being cornered."

As we trampled back up the hill to the front of our tent, we hooted and hollered. Waving our arms as we went. The bear stood up on its back legs to get a better look at us. It decided what bears usually decide, that we weren't worth it's time, and ran off. We collectively put our gear back in the now torn bags and threw in whatever trash the bear left behind.

"How could we be so stupid?" Zeke cried out. "All the pop is gone!"

"For Chrissake!"

"Are you kidding me right now?"

"Jesus Christ, that was the only thing keeping me going!" We all mourned our loss in the same way.

After we collected ourselves, we stowed what was left of our bags into the jeep. I put her in gear and crept down the trail. Rick had the rifle while riding shotgun, fittingly. I didn't expect to see the man, but we had to be ready in case we did. For somewhere in the same forest as us, was the armed murderer. He would be hiding in brush or lurking through the swamps, anywhere he could find to avoid detection.

The camp was hollow. We had never seen it so bare and empty, void of life. It was a city hidden away during the mid-summer season. The beaches and trails were all barren of anyone. The rumble of the engine and the crunch of gravel beneath the tires were the only sounds in the entirety of the reservation. There was no chatter among us. We almost expected to be ambushed by Boone, like a highwayman. Though the further along we went, we grew increasingly confident that he wouldn't show. We drove over the chain that intended on keeping us from entering in the first place. Our endeavor would come to a close, having done all we could.

"We should visit Darlene," Zeke finally said from the back seat. "She'd want to know."

"I don't think so," I challenged. "She needs time to recover. We'd only make it worse. We're gonna drop off the tape and then head home." Zeke then looked out from his side of the car, staring vaguely into the trees as they passed. He never liked when someone turned down an idea of his, though unfortunately he had grown used to it. His earth-brown curls blew in the rush of the wind. "Hey," I got his attention again. "It was a good idea," He nodded and allowed himself to smile.

It wasn't far from when we left camp, where we came across the County Sheriffs building. The old thing could have been picked out of a western. Bared windows and an old wooden sign above the door. I pulled into the lot and dug out the tape that would Boone in the ground.

"Just wait here," I closed the door and walked across the gravel to the office. I heard Zeke get out of the car, but he must have stayed where I asked. The bell rang above the door as I stepped inside the dim building.

"Can I help you?" The man at the desk tapped his cigarette on an ashtray.

"I'm here about the murder of Jay Edgar," I started, having not known what else to say. A few others who were in the small office stopped what they were doing and peered up at me. "I have a recorded confession that a man named Benjamin Taylor was responsible for his death," I held out the cassette. The deputy behind the desk was speechless, but another came up from behind me. "He lives out at Tomahawk Scout Camp, where Jay's body was found."

"Looks like we have a man to hunt down," He said as he grabbed a set of keys. "Come on, boy. You better lead us to him," A few other deputies were getting their jackets on and grabbing their rifles.

"I was hoping you guys would just take it from here," I tried to hand off the recording.

"I don't know if you noticed, but we're pretty short staffed. You want him found? You help find 'em," I read from his badge that his name was Dawson. He was only a deputy but seemed to be strongly taking the initiative.

I got into the jeep and sighed deeply, putting the cassette in my backpack. Something didn't feel right. As the cops got into their cars and turned the sirens on, I whipped around and drove back toward camp. I could see the guys in the rearview mirror, looking at each other, but they soon realized what we were doing. The squad cars processed behind me as we speed back to finish the job.

"He lives in a cabin, a few miles down this trail. It goes out to a road on the other side of camp," I stated as I pulled over on the road near the beach.

"We could flush him out if we push from both sides. He can't easily escape through the lake," One of the deputies added.

"He's armed, just so you know. He'll have bear traps around his shack," Rick added.

"You two," Deputy Dawson pointed at Jack and me. "You'll come with me on this side and lead the way to the cabin. You guys will go with Deputy Ward on the far side. Briggs and Johnson, you'll be on the road parallel to the lake, in case he tries to escape that way," With his orders, we dispersed. I bumped fists with Zeke and Rick before walking to the trail with Jack. We left our cars and went into the brush.

We didn't stick to the trail, which meandered around the shoreline. We fanned out and walked straight through the forest, where the enemy was most likely hiding out. I could feel my adrenaline kicking in again. I needed to end this. I needed this to be over.

"You boys stay close to me, case he sneaks up on us," Dawson let out. "You take it slow," He called to me. I was starting to shake and heat up again from the last chase. "Just take it easy, scan the line slowly as you go," He was right, I needed to keep my head.

Slowing myself down, there was something almost peaceful, yet I knew it was only the calm before the storm. All the pain that had been pushed down would resurface. When the inevitable came, I could finally get my rest. I could finally be free. Boone was a runner, and from what we saw, he had the potential to be a fighter, too. He could have been stalking us from the trees, covered in bones as he silently waited in the branches.

I scanned the horizon slowly as we bushwhacked through the swamp. Ponds would appear here and there to slow us down. Trees kept the forest dark with their wretched limbs and low-hanging moss. Birds coed to each other and the frogs kept the dirt full of sound, too.

"So how did you all find this guy?" Dawson eventually asked.

"We went to camp here, found his shack by accident," Jack said. I suppose lying made the story cleaner, simpler.

"Huh. Yeah, I'm just relieved we finally found the real murderer," He sighed.

"What do you mean the real murderer?" I asked. Jack turned and picked up on what I was thinking.

"You know, we didn't know who the guy was. Now we do," Dawson nodded and kept going. "Ah, isn't this a mess!" He quickly diverted our attention to the marsh in front of us. Water covered the whole forest floor. Humps of land peaked out from the lagoons. "We're catching this son of a bitch," Dawson sighed, stepped into the muck, and continued trudging along. We shrugged and pressed on, going into the black water. Toads would dive into the marsh as we wadded by, slowly making our way.

I had to double take a few times, mistaking oddly shaped trees for our foe. Birds had made nests in some of branches, giving off unnatural structures. Almost like scarecrows, they hauntingly resembled disfigured people. It made me feel small, to be half submerged and having these towering ents surrounding me.

"Anyway, how did you happen to come across that tape? Ya'll weren't trespassing, were ya?" Dawson attempted to make conversation in the dark silence.

"How did you know there was a murderer?" I countered.

"What's that?" He nervously called back.

"You said you knew that there was a murderer."

"Well, obviously the boy was murdered. We all knew that."

"So why did you release that it was an accident?" Dawson turned around, thigh deep in the water. "Why would you say he drowned if you knew that wasn't the truth?" I was horrified to realize the answer to my own question.

"We just didn't want the public to get scared, that's all. Besides we didn't know who the real killer was."

"We didn't, but you did."

"What do you mean?"

"Jay happened across Boone's cabin. He stepped on a bear trap but managed to escape. Boone thought he died on the run, so he confessed to the incident, but maybe that wasn't the whole story," I questioned. Deputy Dawson tightened his grip on the rifle. "Something much worse happened, didn't it? Something that needed to be covered up, something that needed a scapegoat. You didn't have one then, so Jay drowned. But you have one now, a perfect scapegoat with a confession and all, just handed to you," I walked up to him, trying to pry as much as I could. I could tell he was getting uncomfortable. Dawson was shaking his head, quivering. "Can't admit it to yourself? Or can't have anyone know?"

"Shut up!" He spun around; his rifle was pointed at me. "You know nothing," His voice became shaky.

"What did you do?" I knew now we didn't have the full picture before.

"You think I won't kill you right now?" He switched his aim to Jack, then back to me. He was panicking, we had him cornered. "You think I won't do it again?!"

"All to protect your name. You would murder three people to keep your record clean? You are a monster," I spat. I had put all of my focus on the wrong man. Dawson began to shake more, letting tears fall from his eyes, still not coming to terms with what he had done. "How many other cops knew?"

"Oh, no one knew," He shook his head, trembling. "I made sure to take point on his investigation, had everyone convinced he drowned. I was *thorough* that nobody would ever know. Guess I never thought someone from the outside would discover something different," Dawson wiped his eyes and started to breath unevenly. "I was drinking that night, off duty. I got a call, needed a responder to some break-in. I-I was nearby, so I left. I thought I was fine. I barely saw the kid," He started to bawl. "I was going so fast and didn't notice him until it was too late. I had to do something. I couldn't just leave him there!"

"So, you threw him into the lake?" The broken man was crying, ever harder.

"One-just one mess up, I would-would have been done. I would have lost everything! I was-I *am* a good person; I didn't deserve to lose it all over one mistake."

"What about Miss Edgar? Didn't she lose everything?!" I challenged, forgetting I was still at the wrong end of the gun.

"I wasn't thinking! I was drunk!" He screamed. His bloodshot eyes were piercing. His overwhelming guilt and shame turned to rage. "I did what I did. And I could do it again, tell the others *Boone* got you!" He waved his arms.

"Please," I whispered as he brought the gun up to his shoulder. "Please don't shoot."

"He haunts me, you know. I see that boys face everywhere I go," He let out. His cheek against the stock of the gun, his eyes down the sights.

"He haunts me, too. But if you just admit what you've done, then maybe there can be some moving on," I started to tear up in fear. "We can move on."

"I can't live on with this. I thought I could cover it up, but I guess I couldn't. There's only one way," His face lost all of its color. He rotated the rifle until the barrel was under his chin and pulled the trigger.

I gasped and fell to my knees, collapsing into the water. Jack ran to me, putting his arms around me from behind. For a fragile moment, my life was not in my own hands. Jack grabbed my collar and brought me out of the march and yelled for help. I was so lost in myself; I couldn't hear Jack repeatedly asking if I was okay. He put his arm around me and ran us out of the forest, continuing to cry for help until we eventually reached our car.

Jack called for help from the radio in the deputy's car. As sirens eventually overtook the ringing in my ears, my senses too came back to me. Everything was clear to me now. I finally understood the order of events, how everything eventually played out. I understood who really murdered Jay Edgar. I reached for my bag, though I felt someone try to get me to sit back down. I pulled out the tape and staggered over to the water. That damming confession that would put Boone back under the knife was hurled into the lake where it would be buried with the dead. From across the bay, I saw a man who had appeared to have witnessed all that had happened. He turned, what look like to me, then disappeared into the swamp.

Closure

A year had passed, and Rick followed through with his intentions of joining the Marines. He and his father had shipped over to Vietnam to fight the war. So, some dad who didn't know what scouting looked like if it hit him with a train was put in his place as scoutmaster. The rest of us guys were just preparing for another year. I would be going to a college here in town, same as Joe. The others still had their senior year of high school ahead of them.

I had moved on from what had occurred last summer and thought that I would never have to think about it again. But during the last days of the season, when I found myself working at the local gas station, my manager from the front counter yelled out that I got a call. No one was hardly ever inside the store, so I would do no harm to stop stocking shelves for a moment.

"Hello?" I leaned up against the counter.

"Hi, is this Lane?"

"Uh, yeah. What do you need?"

"I'm calling from the Bayshore Retirement home down on park point. A resident told us to call you. Said that you were her grandson and that it was urgent you come to see her, being she's not in good health."

"Hold on, who said this...?"

"Darlene Edgar. I'm sorry, did we dial the wrong number?"

"Oh, uh, no. This is the right number."

"Alrighty. I don't know exactly what she wanted to see you about, but she made it clear to us that it was important you saw her."

"I'll be there," I never thought I would hear that name again or see her again for that matter. After work, I took off my apron and went out to my car. I didn't know what to expect when I got down there. It was still such a hard topic to talk about. The drive down didn't take long, passing by the ever-familiar buildings, driving this route into Duluth was almost automatic. There was a fair amount of traffic down by the canal, it was still hot that day. I passed by Bayshore going to and from the beaches on Park Point, but I'd never been inside. It looked like an apartment building that was only a few stories high. I walked into the lobby, which smelled like a hospital, and asked the lady at the desk where I could find Darlene's room. She led me down the series of halls, talking about how wonderful the patients were the whole way. She knocked on the door and slowly walked inside. Even the rooms looked like hospital rooms.

"Miss Edgar, your grandson is here to see you," I saw from the door frame that she was sitting in the corner watching the news with a blanket over her lap. She did not look well. I walked in as the nurse left the room.

"Turn off that tv, son," She muttered. Her voice was faint. I switched it off and went to sit in a chair next to her. "They only allow family in here, so I'm sure you know why I had to lie."

"Understandable."

"This place is a lot worse than the brochure made it out to be," She pointed to a copy on the table. The cover had an iconic picture of a Lake Superior view on it. "Haven't seen the lake since I've been here. Been weeks since I've been outside."

"Why's that?"

"The people here, some of them have issues. They yell and yell to get the nurses' attention, so they cater to their every need. But those of us who are more composed get forgotten. I can't walk hardly anymore, but none of the caretakers ever check on me. I've been pinned in front of that tv for days," She shook her head. "Would you mind taking me outside? I think I'll need some fresh air."

I nodded and helped her up. She was a lot weaker since I saw her last. I brought her walker to her and helped her out of the room and down the hall. We got to a set of doors which were locked and had to wait for the nurse to open them to let us outside. To keep patients from trying escape I had guessed. We got to the courtyard, which was walled as high as the building itself.

"The lake's right there," She pointed at the prison wall. "No windows even face it," I grew ever disturbed of this retirement building that people pay lots of money to live in. We went and sat on a bench in the small yard. Darlene sat there for a moment and just closed her eyes and breathed. "You boys are smart," She turned to me. "I knew that from when you came to my house. I know you know what happened. The police gave up on the case from day one, but I knew that you would continue on. I knew you, having such a burden for my boy, would carry on," She paused. "This is going to be hard, but I want you to tell me. Tell me everything, in whatever way you can. I'm dying, Lane and I can't go without knowing what happened to my Jay," There was hurt in her eyes and I shared that hurt with her. Only her knowing those long passed events would put her to ease. My eyes began to shed tears. I composed myself and looked up at her. I told her everything that had happened. Told her last summer caused a lot of boys to grow up really quick. I told her I hadn't been in camp five minutes, the time I found the body.

Book Two
Homeaiming

Clairvoyant

Exodus

W hat if we left?" Zeke said to me, keeping his soft gaze on the cityscape below. The air was hot and still, not even the highway under our feet made a comprehensible sound. I took my time to respond, thinking carefully.

"We've been over this, man," I eventually shook my head lightly.

"But what if we *actually* left."

"Zeke," I turned to him from the driver seat, about to lecture.

"I mean it this time, Lane. No more fables, no more reminiscing. I want to leave."

"How many ties would we cut? We are so anchored down; we couldn't leave even if wanted to. Who would allow us to do that? What about my job or our families?"

"That's where you're wrong. We have this illusion that we are tied down here, but we aren't. The world doesn't hold dominion over us. We can physically just get up and leave whenever we want. Life isn't a road; we aren't stuck on the track. We can go off the common path, and if we don't like what we see, we can always come back on."

"It's not that simple, Zeke. If we leave, there isn't a return. We can't just start over."

"Maybe you're right, but I'm willing to make that sacrifice. I could give up all of this; society. And I know you could do!"

"Think about what you're saying. Because it isn't a lighthearted move. This is a huge commitment that neither of us would be ready for. We are making a decision that will haunt us the rest of our lives. We're planning for a future longer than what we've even lived."

"And college? Can you say you haven't made changes that would affect the rest of your life? We've been groomed to believe that's the only way the road goes. That working some lame job after college is the only acceptable route in our lives, and it's not. Sure, we've gone to school to prepare us for college and we've gone to college to prepare us for a job, but what then? That boring office job prepares us for retirement, which prepares us for death. It doesn't end. That track isn't living. It's muting. It is meant to mute and tame any personality you have, so much that you become a machine. Your only purpose is to push buttons, count numbers. I want more than that. Tell me you don't. Because if I know you at all, you would hate to see your life wash away like this."

"And *if* you're wrong?"

"Then I put twenty-five years of faith into the wrong person," He shot me. I hated how glib he was. He always knew which strings to pull.

I drove him back from where we were parked. We didn't speak a lick to each other, however his final words still stuck out of my chest like an arrow. It almost killed me to think that I, even for a moment, believed Ezekiel to be wrong. He was my brother, as much as the rest of the gang, he knew me inside and out. At the end of the day, his assumptions about me would always be right. He knew every thought in my brain. Even now, I knew how serious he was this time. He certainly knew that if he actually left, I would surely follow. He just wanted me to be on his side, wholly.

My parents would have been the ones to on carry after me. I couldn't do that to them. I moved out of the house eight years ago and yet, they would be destroyed had I left for good. If I left, it would have to seem accidental. As if I simply went out on a hike and never returned. But to *never* return, that's a daunting concept. I tended not to miss things when I was away from home. I never got homesick, but only because I knew I would one day come back. I can't say I know the feeling to be so wayward as to never come back again.

I wanted to say Zeke was wrong about society. I wanted more than anything to be right this time, but he made a point I couldn't ignore. The fact that society was manufactured to tame us. Man was created in the wilderness. We were all born wild animals, but quickly become cultured to act as stoic as the machines we built. Perhaps a machine is left in the wild, would it return to its untamed state? Or would it rust and decay, resisting the vines that start to grow around it, remain autonomous until it's death? I spent all my life learning to be civilized, subconsciously. Would it ever be possible for a civilized man to become feral? I feared both outcomes for myself and for my brother. Should I remain in an urban state of mind, I won't survive off the earth. Should I turn undomesticated, I have no idea who I will become. I turned it over in my mind until I turned myself over to sleep.

"Let's go on a hike," Zeke called me from my apartment telephone.

"Now? I have work today," I paused, still in bed. "What time is it?"

"Four thirty."

"Jesus, Zeke. Can't we go this weekend?"

"What was it you used to say? 'The tides of time wait for no man'?"

"Well, the tides of *you* are going to have to wait," I hung up. "I know what you're up to," I said to myself.

I liked life after college so far. Living away from home, making steady money, and meeting a girl occasionally. I don't think Zeke was so established in his life to realize what he was asking me to give up. And what of our friends? Everyone was still in Duluth. The rest of our group would be losing their jock and the guy with the best hair. Two very crucial members to any gang. "Why couldn't they all come with?" I often wondered. Why was it that Zeke wanted to make it personal; that the crusade was to be exclusively his and mine?

That Saturday morn, I drove to his childhood house. He was already standing out in his driveway, with a backpack easily twice his size. I pulled over near him on the gravel road. Besides him and I, crows were the only other beings awake.

"Got enough stuff there?" I questioned.

"Only what we need," He said with a smirk. I chose not to say anything to him after that, not until we made it to the trailhead.

"Is this really what we want? Now just isn't the time, Zeke," I put the old jeep in park and turned off the engine.

"Adventure doesn't wait until we're ready. It takes us by the wrist and pulls us wherever it wants. We could resist and fall, or we can let it take us. Let the world decide our lives from there. See where adventure takes you!"

"Adventure isn't the one pulling," I got out of the car. "You are."

"Maybe I am, but then I'm just a catalyst for what the world wants. Mother Nature's prophet," Zeke hulled his pack out from the trunk and started to make his way for the trail. I didn't move.

"Zeke," I muttered, still leaning against the car. Ezekiel kept on walking. "At least let me carry the pack!" I called out to him. He could barely lift it, let alone hike the trail with it.

"Thank God!" I didn't know if he was excited about me hiking with him or carrying the backpack. "I'll tell you what, Lane. We just hike out for night, cause that's what we said we would do. If we choose to go back then we can, but if we choose to stay, we already have everything we need," He gestured to the pack that was over my shoulder.

"Okay."

We went out from the trailhead. Leaving the vermillion red Cherokee as the only trace we were ever there. It would look exactly as it was, to anyone investigating. If we did leave, it would look like we just went out for a hike and never returned. We got lost and our bodies were never found.

"Never" is a long time, I've come to realize. It's not like I would returning in another twenty-six years. It was hard enough to fathom time longer than I've been alive. Never lasts for all of time, there is no going back, for as long as I live and beyond that. I didn't look back, though. I looked ahead, to see Zeke parading us into the wilderness. Realistically, this was it. I *did* want to see if we could live in the forests, like we thought about for so long.

Zeke was right about everything, maybe not that the planet worked through him, but he knew I wanted this too. As much as I tried to be reasonable, I feel he could easily win this. We all got grounded after coming back from our stunt at Tomahawk, but we're not kids anymore. We would have real world consequences. We wouldn't see the end of it, not until the day we die.

When hiking, each of us mainly kept to our thoughts. Our inability to talk for hours didn't mean we weren't close. We could always see through each other and knew exactly what's going on inside. I could tell Zeke was nervous. He was in charge now, not me. In the city streets, I was our ringleader, but not here. This was his undertaking, from now on it would be him calling the shots. He had to be the watchman.

I could see he was rethinking his decision, maybe it dawned on him that this was actually happening. He had been talking about the wilds for so long, but once he opened the door to step into it, what he saw scared him. All of this he hid under his cheerful pep. There's a noticeable difference between genuine enthusiasm and the kind of spirit a man displays when he isn't wholehearted. Zeke wanted to believe in his own cause, for he needed me to believe in it. But I could tell beneath his skin, he was scared.

Camp was set up near dusk. Zeke took the liberty of showing me everything I had been carrying for the past day. There were sleeping bags for each of us, spare layers of clothes, hunting knives, flint and steel, a moderate first-aid kit, nonperishable food, and plenty of rope.

Rope was by far the most valued possession we had. It wasn't hard for us Eagle Scouts to bring objects into creation with a fistful of good line. Shelters, platforms, tools, traps, nets; if it existed, we could Swiss-Family-Robinson-it. Zeke also managed to stuff an axe and a collapsible shovel into the pack. Explains why my back was killing me. The axe would serve not only as a useful tool, but also our only line of protection.

I thought briefly to myself that having a good stock of equipment was cheating. Although, Zeke was the one making the game. He deemed it fair to have enough supplies to establish ourselves, for our only adversary had an endless arsenal. Nature could unleash anything on us, without warning, simply to display her superiority over mankind. Her ways are random, unpredictable, and yet, fair.

Humanity found a way to kill her slowly, suffocate her with toxins, which had convinced them that they could outlast her. Men told themselves they were the apex overall. They lose that "primitive internal," as I've heard it called. They forgot how powerful she really is. Which leaves me troubledly undecided on the debate. Is man really master of all? Or does the Earth still hold reign over her subjects?

I didn't sleep that entire night. I might have faded in and out of life, but I got no rest. I knew what the morning sun meant. I knew it was time to decide our fate. It was time to sign our lives away. All for a cause we didn't even understand. Enlist in the army of ourselves to fight the war on survival.

We rolled up our nap sacks and gathered everything back into the bag I would carry. Zeke started down the trail, yet I stayed right where I was.

"Zeke," He turned back to me. "That's the wrong way," He smiled. Yet, I couldn't see whether he meant to walk back to where we came or if it was by accident. He patted my shoulder as he walked past. Leading us with his head held high, I could tell now, he was more at ease with his plan. We would be going off into the wild.

The day was crisp and the jacket I packed didn't quite fulfill its duty at keeping me warm. It would have been better, had there not been that breeze blowing through the evergreens. We abandoned the trail not long into the walk. If someone were to come looking for us, the path was where they would look. If we really wanted to vanish, we needed to get a considerable distance from any man-made establishment. If we wanted to disappear, we needed to actively run from humanity.

The forest here was thick and full of ferns, which blended the ground into the trees seamlessly. Minnesota forests were always overgrown with stubborn saplings and filled with every kind of bug that nature cooked up. I didn't want to know how many ticks were already leaching onto me.

Due north was the approximate direction we were heading. By day we kept our bearings by the sun, and by night we looked for the North Star. The hiking trail followed the North Shore of the lake, which ran southwest to northeast. We were gradually distancing ourselves from old *Gitchi-Gami*. The cross-section map of the region looked like a sawblade, which gives the range its name, the Sawtooth Mountains. The elevation changed so frequently, as if the land rippled out from the lake's great waves. This made trailblazing more strenuous.

I thought deep about what we were doing. At what point would our decision become irreversible? How far could we tread before we lost our way back? We pushed further into the belly of the beast. She has swallowed more skillful men than us, breaking the spirits of braver men. The frontier unfolded before us, taking us in. She knew all she had in store for us and intended to keep her plot a secret.

We broke for lunch near a creek that dribbled across the granite terrain. My spine was starting to go numb from carrying the pack. With all the weight in the bag, the one thing not terribly accounted for, was food. We had a fair number of non-perishables; granola, dried fruit, and beef jerky.

"We're going to need to start fishing," I spoke up, gazing into the water beneath my feet. "Hunting and gathering, too. Before we run out of food."

"Okay, we haven't exactly had much to hunt with. We could make rodent traps with the rope we have, but other than that, we're pretty limited."

"I know we're limited. That's why I'm expressing my concern. Fishing is going to be our best source of food. We could follow this and see if it gets bigger downstream. Worst case scenario, we end up back at the Lake," I swatted at a mosquito.

"There are roads and people all along the shore, we couldn't go back there without crossing back into society."

"Does that outweigh starving to death? Are we really going to test ourselves to *that* extreme?" I asked Zeke.

"I mean, isn't that the point?" He asked. "To see just how long we could last? You had to have known this only ends with nature eating us up, one way or another. I would personally rather die lost in the woods, than of old age after living a boring, mediocre life. You should have been well aware of that sacrifice, Lane."

"I am, and I'm sorry if that disturbs me, but I'm not ready to die, yet."

"Well then let's hope we both learned something from Wilderness Survival badge," He got up to press onward into the bush. I took my time getting the bag packed up again.

He thought us missionaries, going into a foreign land to preach a religion that was outlawed, and we would be put to death for it. We came into natures fold, proclaiming the gospel of man; being dominant over her. She would make us pay, one way or another. Our church of two, as Zeke often called us, would end right then and there. No one around to examine or testify what we died for. We would be martyred, hanged on a tree as heretics, for all of nature's subjects are devote followers of her doctrine. She is goddess overall; she designed the equilibrium in which all things exist. Humanity threw a wrench in her whole system and now we came to spit in her face.

How could we expect to live long out here?

Natural Selection

Ever tried spear fishing?" Zeke brought forth his creation. We called it a spear, but it was little more than a fashionable stick.

"Can't say I have, what was the rule with the refraction? Aim above or below the fish?" I was washing my shirt in the large brook.

"I believe it's below," He confirmed. "And I believe I am going to catch one!" He plunged the spear into the water, trying to balance on a rock that protruded from the river.

"Keep telling yourself that, if we made a trap or net, we could catch significantly more."

"What's the sport in that?" Zeke laughed.

"The sport is that we get to eat today!" I called back, then chuckled to myself. Ezekiel was naturally skinny, so he hadn't been taking the rationing too badly. I, on the other hand, was noticeably losing weight and I felt the hunger pains far more than he did. I was burning considerably more calories than he was since he was not carrying the backpack.

While Zeke was trying out his spear, I decided to try for some smaller game. Kicking over rocks and sifting around in the water, galvanized black darts to shoot from one cover to the next. Crawfish are moderately easy to catch, being that they only swim backwards and can only see in front of them. We got plenty of experience at scout camps, catching and boiling crawfish.

It seemed I was still in good practice, catching one within minutes. I taunted its pincers with my finger, letting the creature think it could pinch me.

"Uh, where should we put what we catch?" I turned about in the water, looking for a container in our camp. The damn thing got me in my distraction. "Shit," I tried to flick it off. Zeke hopped on rocks out of the creek and dug out a pot from the pack. He drew water and placed it on the rugged shore, next to me. "Mad that you couldn't spear a fish?" I prodded. He shook his head as he went back to his task, in denial.

We've been gone five days now. No telling what our families are going through. No doubt they found the jeep. Zeke and I both told our parents where we would be hiking; we looked more like a disappearance than a run-away. I'm sure once the news got out that Ezekiel and I went missing on a hike, the rest of the gang would immediately know exactly what happened. They knew how we talked about leaving, going way out in the woods, they would know without a second thought we actually did it.

We boiled what we had for dinner that night; a handful of crawfish as well as wild raspberries for dessert. Not that our packed food was gone, we just had every intention of making it last. Zeke took his canteen and raised it high.

"A toast! To the lost boys who know exactly their place in the world."

"The adventure never truly begins until we're lost," I raised my cup in compliance. It was freeing, being out in the frontier of nature. I still held onto the gravity of our decision. "What do you think the rest of the *lost boys* are doing right now?"

"Our friends?" Zeke asked. "They're probably out looking for us."

"You think so? I would assume they moved on. I mean, they knew this is what we wanted, why try to bring us back?"

"For the sake of having us back. Because, our gang doesn't survive divided."

"So, why'd you divide us?" He didn't respond. "If you truly believe that the gang won't carry on after we've left, why cause us to leave?"

"I suppose it was inevitable. We were destined to do this, and they weren't."

"Don't give me that destiny, shit," I threw a rock at Zeke. "You choose for us to do this on your free will. You choose for it to be just us and not them."

"No one else would have remotely considered, that's why in the end, it was just us. No one else is stouthearted like we are."

"Don't disrespect them for wanting to stay in society and make something of themselves. You know they have just as brave of hearts as us. If anything, they are the better ones, for they took the confines of civilization and shaped it to fit their beliefs. We just ran away from it. They have the lion hearts, not us, because they stayed and fought against everything they hated about the world. They ran toward the society that threw them down, we abandoned the ship."

"Do you regret leaving?" Zeke shot at me.

"Look at how we're living, Zeke," I sighed. "We're hardly eating, we exist between campfires, living hand to mouth. Don't pretend that this is glorious. You wanted to be kings; look at us! We're peasants."

"The Israelites struggled for forty years before finding the promise land. You need to find the faith to get through. You're wanting to go back to Egypt but believe me when I say we will find our promise land. We will be kings there! Just believe in me, Lane. Please," His frustration with me turned into passion.

I sat with Ezekiel's words as he left the fire to go to his tiny shelter. Eventually, my own sleeping bag found a way to call me in for the night.

"Lane," Zeke softly called later. I grunted in acknowledgement. "Would you die for me?"

"What?"

"Would you die for me? We always said that we would die for our brothers, but out here that possibility is a lot more prevalent. I just want to reaffirm that you *would* give up your life for me, because I would bleed just as much for you."

"I already gave up my life for you, Zeke."

My mind turned over what Zeke had said to me earlier. Perhaps he had a hint of truth in his claims; that somewhere there was a promised kingdom for us.

The sun snuck through the woven branches just enough to wake us the next morning. We became very efficient at packing camp and setting it up later on. The faster we could make and break camp, the more time on the road. Wanderers before kings, that was the idea Zeke was planting in me.

The creek we found most likely flowed south into Lake Superior, so we decided to travel against the current, leading us further into desolation. Upstream also meant that what little river we had would probably be getting smaller. This would dissipate our only tangible source of food.

As we walked through the forest, the ground grew to stone-cut cliffs and the soil sank down into ponds. Moss and tiny ferns grew on the boulders, contrasting a deep green with the light grey ore. We followed the bottom of the canyon, hiding in the light mist that ascended from the streams and pools. Red pines grew in abundance in this gentle gully. No birds were singing, no wind was blowing in this neck of the forest, just tiny moths fluttering between ferns. It wasn't an eerie silence, though, as if we were being stalked by a mountain lion. This was a calm, restful silence. We felt safe on the path, which was wide and green with life.

A prehistoric tree grew out from the side of the rock. Its trunk hunched over into an arch. The spiny branches stuck out like spikes on a dinosaur's back. The behemoth grazed in the fields of ferns. Like an ancient guardian, the pine would remain, watching over the canyon for eternity.

We were home-aiming at this point. Searching through the wilderness for a promised kingdom. There had to be a verb or abstract noun to describe it. I couldn't pin the emotion, but I felt now that I was approaching the inevitable. As if I could almost hear the triumphant applause of thousands as the long-awaited brother-kings finally returned home. A *fernweh*, a longing for where we haven't been yet.

"Saunterer," I found my word.

"What was that?" Zeke called back to me, hearing my thoughts out loud.

"Saunter. The word comes from, *a la sainte terre,* meaning 'to the Holy Land.' Therefore, we are saunterers. Just like you were saying."

"I know you didn't come up with that yourself."

"No, John Muir did," I confirmed. In that moment, I felt a shift. I had once believed that we were walking into the depth of the unknown, into the heart of the antagonist and away from the safety of civilization. Now, what's behind is the hallow darkness. What lays ahead is the warm, royal welcome. Society will be just fine without us.

Night came fast on us. Ezekiel and I made our camp as per usual. Each of us having a shelter on differing sides of a central campfire. The bright amber sparks faded into the navy sky, joining the stars. As I was greeted by the fire's heart, I was reminded that warm weather isn't a luxury that lasts forever in Minnesota. Eventually we would have to dig in for the winter, hibernate if we had to. It wasn't one of those "cross that bridge when we get there" situations. Winter would mean death if we weren't ready well in advance. It was nearly stalking us as we huddled around our fire. It was waiting in the weeds for the proper time to strike. It sneered at us for clinging onto the warmth that we thought could protect us.

I seized myself awake at the sound of a loon. We hadn't realized we were camped so close to a lake, harboring fields of wild rice. The bird, whose banshee cry could be heard across the hemisphere, was now my mortal enemy. It was too damned early to be woken up. I then found several large stones to hurl it. Scaring it away, cursing its existence, and giving it the middle finger was all I needed to do to be filled with satisfaction. Zeke still sound asleep in his hut, twigs growing from his mangled hair. I hit him as I walked by to start packing up camp.

As I began up the unpaven path, I noticed Ezekiel wasn't following. Turning back, I saw him stacking the rocks we used to make the fire pit. I studied him silently. Each stone was strategically placed to make the form of a man.

"It's an *Inukshuk,*" Zeke pointed at his creation. These stone men were often used to mark trails. "If we are to leave any trace on this planet, it should be our journey. That will be our legacy. These markers will tell our story, if anyone were to follow them in ten thousand years," I nodded to him, approving his idea.

The Kingdom

Hiding among the thistles and crooked roots, two iron beams emerged. They ran alongside each other and dove in and out of the earth. Only by means of chance, could they be discovered.

"What the-" I nearly tripped over the beam. "Zeke, take a look at this!" I called to him, who had passed over unaware. "Railroad," Both our eyes lit as we looked up to see the tracks swim into the pines.

"Let's see where it goes," Zeke changed his heading and went up the line. The steel rods were rusted and were being gnawed at by plant-folk of all kind. Ferns and saplings all eating away at the man-made obstruction. We found it difficult to follow the tracks, being that large portions were under ground. I can't say that we didn't get lost a few times, but we always found our way back again.

The further we treaded, the more prevalent the tracks became. Crossbeams were starting to emerge. We even passed over a bridge, barely holding itself in suspension. The pine trees were growing darker, not in a sinister way, rather as if they were preparing for sleep with the dusk.

"It almost feels like old times," Zeke chuckled as we prepared a fire on the tracks. The hardy axe cut through wood with ease, which was always a favorite activity of mine when we broke for camp.

"A bit," I wiped my brow and went to chopping more logs. It was easy to reminisce on passed days with the gang. There was a larger chorus then, but we were none the less strong.

My eyes opened softly to find the grass staring at me. I sat myself up to realize both Zeke and I fell asleep, cuddled around the fire. Brushing the dirt from my fleece, I got up and took a walk. From the distance, I saw that the tracks weren't just ours, but deer used them as well. In the morning dew they passed like mist, they were so quiet, weightlessly floating along.

The crunch of my boots didn't seem to startle them. It was always my innate quest to see how close I could get before scaring the poor things off. Stags were majestic in nature, something in me felt as if I needed to earn their respect. Like they were the ancient protectors of the land. Eventually, my presence repelled them back into the dark. I had gotten close enough to see what they were gathered around: wild blueberries.

"Found some breakfast," I held up my handfuls of fruit. Zeke didn't seem too concerned with my absence. He was preparing another cairn of rocks to leave behind. We shared what I had found, and would no doubt stop for more when we would pass the bushes again. "How much of the food we packed do we have left?"

"Not a lot. A bit granola, maybe some jerky."

"Dammit."

"Yeah, we're going to need to start hunting and gathering more," Zeke stated what we both knew.

"We can't exactly hunt with an axe and a shovel."

"I know that. Let's just see if the tracks lead us to another river, fishing seemed like the most reliable source of food."

"Alright," I nodded. Ezekiel led the charge onward. Even being on the most remote set of tracks, I still was subconsciously nervous that a phantom train would come and run us down.

As we treaded onward, Zeke began to habitually look to his right. I tried to follow where he was looking, but I couldn't see anything.

"You alright?" I questioned him. He veered off the tracks and went into the forest. "Zeke," I was hesitant to run after him. "Zeke!"

"Hold on, Lane," He chipped back. Eventually he stopped his course. "Do you see it?" I humored him and scanned the horizon of pines.

"No, what is it?" He pointed into the oblivion of the woods. I shifted next to him, put my head on his shoulder to match his finger to my eyeline. Beyond the deep jade branches and the foliage that speared out of the ground, a white post. It stood unapologetically in the middle of the vast, grainy wilderness.

"What do you think that is?" Zeke asked me.

"A sign maybe. Narnia?"

"Well, let's go found us a faun," The young man trampled through the rooted ground toward the isolated object. I followed his lead as per usual. Paint was well cracked on the post, it seemed as ancient as the railroad tracks. On the ground was a sign that the beam should have been holding up. I wiped off as much dirt as possible, but I still couldn't make out where the sign was welcoming us to. "Lane, look up," I was hit on the shoulder.

"Holy shit," I laughed with excitement. Ahead of us was a town, hiding under vines. I could see now, a road making way to plants who refused to stop growing. Where man had once established themselves, nature was slowly closing in her fist.

We were pulled into the forgotten Iron Range town, captivated by its story. What unsung tales were buried with this town? To my right was a storefront, whose windows had been smashed in. Crows inside were picking at a dead rodent. No food seemed to be left behind. Whoever was here, took everything when they left.

Glass cracked behind me. I turned sharply to see Zeke stepping on a broken window near a ruined house. He unfastened the door and disappeared in the musty shade. Knowing he could take care of himself, I ventured alone down the street. The one road appeared to be the extent of the little village, with narrow avenues that branched out like ribs. There was a gas station next door, along with several other houses. Brooding above it all, was an iron water tower. It kept watch over its land, its spirit was worn from seeing the humble town slowly crumble to its death.

The gas station was surprisingly inviting for how crippled it was. The faded blue and red exterior was almost hopeful. Time had eaten away at what merchandise the store would have sold. I was more disheartened that there wasn't a single carbonated drink left, than I was sustainable food. Moldy cigs were all I was able to scavenge, but they were of little use or interest to us. I wish I knew enough about architecture to tell what timeframe this town was from. There were no identifying features on anything that would give myself the slightest clue. I checked to see if the pumps were still working, it was no mystery they weren't.

As I moved on from the station, I heard Zeke trample out of the first house.

"Find anything?" He called from behind me.

"Nothing, you?"

"Yeah," Zeke sighed to himself with content. "I did." I looked back to see him parading a glass bottle. As he marched closer, I could see there was a dark liquid inside the crystal-like container.

"Is that-"

"Whiskey!" Zeke finished the words from my mouth. He and I weren't big into alcohol, still preferring our ritualistic bottle of soda in our adult age.

"Might as well," I laughed.

We scaled to the top of the water tower, naturally. There was a mentality where if something existed, it could be conquered. Zeke and I lived that mentality. Climb every mountain just because it's there, not to feel superior than it, but for sport.

"This is it," Ezekiel turned to me from where we were sitting.

"This is what?"

"Look up," He hit my shoulder. I did as he wanted. Great hills rolled into one another, with the full and healthy pines covering them like grass. The warm evening radiated from the deep sky; birds rejoiced in their song. The view was immaculate, it was royal. Outside of town, a silo stuck out from the forest. A tree had grown straight from the top, growing taller than those around.

"The Promise Land," I smirked.

"Aye. This is our kingdom, Lane," He stood and gave out a howl, which echoed into all horizons. "We are your kings now!" Zeke bellowed from the roof of the tower. I chuckled at my brother, who eventually pulled me up with him. "Long live the kings," He took hold of my shoulder.

"Long live the kings!" I chanted as loud as he had before. We displayed our bravado for the world to know who their rulers were. Zeke broke open the whiskey and took a generous swig. He immediately coughed it out. I laughed a good bit at him, as did he. The whiskey then met my throat. I forced it down, but not without winching a little. It burned more than I expected. "Now that's living," We chuckled to ourselves as we sat on the brim of the tower, dangling out legs in the air. Zeke took the bottle back from me and tried to get the strong drink down a second time. This go around he took a more cautious sip and was, by all standards, successful.

We shared the bottle as the night overtook the day. At this state, when we sang, we thought we sounded better than usual. Though I swore *The Ballad of Davy Crocket* had more than one verse that repeated seven times. It was almost difficult to notice how cold the air was, being that hot coals warmed our insides. However, we eventually called it quits and stumbled back to the ground.

I don't reckon I would have woken up the next morning if it weren't for the ungodly headache that overcame me. I could hear in Zeke's moaning, it had him too. Work seemed like the only thing that could distract my body from the drunkenness that hung over from the previous night.

I made my way to a house nearby and after some inspection, began stripping the trim from the door.

"What are you doing?" An overly annoyed voice came about. Zeke didn't care to move, or even look, from where he was laying.

"Getting wood for a big fire," I pulled the decayed boards from their host. "A big, undying, communal fire. Because if this is to be our-" I grunted as I yanked another board. "-kingdom, it is an absolute necessity to have an eternal flame!"

"Well, yeah. I agree, but could you maybe try making your ceremonial flame a bit quieter?"

"Get yourself some water or find something to do, it might do ya some good," I suggested. After some clear existential struggle, Ezekiel forced himself from the ground. Even in the comfort of his old home, he was never a fan of waking up early.

Opening the door in front of me, I peered inside to see if there was anything left that could be salvaged for firewood. Soggy furniture and molded walls did not make the cut. Even the boarded-up windows were too waterlogged to be burned. I took what I could get: a coatrack, a dresser, and some more trim from the baseboards. All this was piled up to make a grand barricade in the streets. It looked like we were taking reign by revolution.

"You're going to burn all that? We would be seen from Mexico," Zeke waved at my woodpile.

"Not all at once, but it's nice to have everything condensed," I tried my best to persuade Zeke that I wasn't going to start a massive fire that could potentially burn down the forest. He didn't seem to buy it.

"Well, while you gather wood, I may take a look around the area and see if there's a source of water nearby," Zeke walked down one of the alleys and was swallowed by the thick brush.

I continued to scrap and chop wood from the houses, swinging the axe through established walls. Subtly, the hair on the back of neck went into a fringe. There was something unsettling about the ghost town. Lonely isolation wasn't what scared me. The void of life was replaced by another presence. Something unseen and intangible dwelt here. As if its evil presence drove every living thing from the ground. Not even our royal confidence could banish the aura. This, I only noticed when I was alone.

I was, in the simplest sense, the muscle of the old group. Yet, I felt more vulnerable than ever without my comrade. Which gave me an understanding I hadn't come to realize until now. Zeke needed me to come with him on his expedition, otherwise he would have *always* felt this alone. I found some comfort in that, this mutual reliance he and I had on each other.

Footsteps echoed from a location not yet known. I assumed it was Ezekiel. The thin stature and gentle presence given off matched his. The figure had the same shaggy, chestnut hair and dark eyes. But after a moment, I understood that it was a deer. A gorgeous buck strutted down the road where I was on my knee. Its bone crown demanded respect. How folly I was to assume I was a ruler of this forest. Far more appropriate for me to be already kneeling before his majesty.

The deer noticed me and studied me intently. It began to walk toward me now; its hooves clipped on the pavement how steel would meet steel. What force drew it near me, I dare not know. He looked down on me with his gently strong eyes. The closer he approached, the more I got the sense that he was after some form of response. The stag would be disappointed in me if I cowered further, or if I ran. In the face of a king, it would only be just if I stood tall.

I slowly raised myself from the dirt, keeping my gaze on him. The buck stopped his march a few strides from where I stood in a solemn pride. I then, did the only thing I felt it instinctual to do, I bowed. He lifted his head slowly, keeping his eyes fixed on me, then the deer bowed in return. I remained calm, yet at the same time astonished in all that had happened.

The stag turned his head to the soft snap of a twig. I looked as well to see Zeke totally frozen in the brush. With a sigh, the deer turned and walked back into the green wood.

"What was that?" Zeke asked me.

"I think that this city already has a king. I don't think it needs two more," I put my arm around him. "We should move on; this kingdom is well off on its own."

As I packed our belongings into the bag, Zeke reached in and pulled out the axe.

"Woah, whatcha doing with that?" I questioned.

"I got this feeling as I was out today. I don't know, I think maybe it would be best if we had our protection on hand."

"For sure," I knew he had experienced the same feeling of desolation I had earlier. Ezekiel grabbed the straps of the backpack from me and handed me the axe. "You're finally gonna carry the bag, huh?"

"We both know *that* is more your area of expertise," He pointed to the bladed tool. I wasn't fond of my reputation of being the violent one every now and then, but out here in the wild, aggression could mean survival.

"What do we call this place?" I called out to Zeke who had walked past me.

"Serenity," He turned back and proclaimed without question. I nodded in contentment.

After building his stone man, Ezekiel lead us off and not in the way we came. I assume he wanted a wilder approach. We went with instinct and went into the North.

Clairvoyant

Autumn

Ferns flickered, not how the wind might take them, but by the base. Something living was afoot. Its movements could easily be seen by any waiting predator, leaving a ripple of leaves wherever it went. Surrendering from cover, a dark rabbit leapt into the open. It skittered along the soil. Its nose dragging it close to bits of fruit and crumbs left as an offering. A net sprung into the air. The creature with it.

"Get it, Lane!" Zeke shouted as he pulled down on the rope. I charged from the log I was hiding beneath and hit the net with the raw end of the axe. Eventually there was no longer movement from within.

Skinning a rabbit was never something permitted in the Boy Scouts, nor was actually surviving in the wilderness for that matter. The skills we learned were for getting out of emergencies, not intended as a way of life. It took Zeke and I several tries to perfect the rodent trapping scheme, several more to perfect the cooking process.

At this point neither of us guys cared where the meat came from, we just wanted it back in our diet again. Hunger was still an ongoing battle in our lives. We found plenty of water, collecting rain when it fell, but food was hard to come by. The farther north we traveled, the less edible vegetation we found. What was most damning, is that starvation eats at muscle before fat.

We had been following game trails for a week or two now. Though we never saw any deer, nor did we really know how to kill one should we find them. Hiking became more difficult, not that the path was harder to tread, but our bodies were simply weaker. Our legs and feet grew numb to the endless hours of walking. Our belts barely fit anymore. Our fires were burning out.

I couldn't help to feel we had no control, no authority over the Earth. Zeke kept his chin up, but I often wondered of his heart. He was outwardly filled, but inwardly he could be just as broken as I sometimes find myself. He never would let it slip that he had regrets, but I can't help to feel as if he may. Through all the rain and struggle, we're still here. We still lasted longer than some, we still overcame nature to this point. Have we not wrestled with the world and prevailed? If we are kings, we are the ones who carry on passed death. The ones who keep ruling, reluctantly. The planet still had relentless battles for us, even though we have died in our will to reign. I suppose-

"Oh, sorry," I ran into Zeke, not noticing he was frozen before me. "What is…" I looked up from my thoughts to see a pile of ivory. "…it?"

There before us lay a body who had been dead for many years. There was nothing left except the gritty white skeleton, leaning against a stump. Seeing the skull of another human being burned into me. Its blank expression weighed more than any living emotion I had experienced. I felt as if I was back in time, as if I was once again standing on the shore of Long Lake, watching Jay Edgar be taken out of the waters. Once again seeing Boone shoot at Rick and me. Once again seeing the deputy who took his own.

These bones could have been anyone. They could have been me, or Zeke, or one of the guys. This was someone's son or daughter laying before us; this unidentified corpse had a life full of meaning and emotion, and Nature took that away. It ate away at this human as it did with the town we found. The loss of this person's story was perhaps most daunting. It didn't matter who they were, Mother Nature does not discriminate. She takes without evaluation or judgment. Taking only though, their story and identity, and spitting out the most primal remains: the bones.

Only the birds can sing about what happened after we pass on in the wild. The trees alone are left to tell the story. Like bards they recall the tales of what epic events had taken place, but there was no ear on Earth to hear them. No one would be able to understand the language of the trees.

"Let's burry 'em," Zeke muttered, turning away. "It isn't right for their body to be spread across the ground."

"Okay," I softly agreed. We dug with the spade, a trench for the bones to be laid in. Something didn't feel right about moving each piece of ivory, but we both agreed the body needed to be buried intact. So, one by one, we moved each bone of this corpse; placing them diligently in their correct orientation. The skull was the last to be moved, I feared it more than anything. To touch the head would be touching the hollow shell of the soul. "I can't," I turned to Ezekiel.

"It's alright, Lane," He coughed and rubbed my shoulder, then went down and pinched the skull by the temples and cradled the jaw with his other hand. He set it down as if this person was resting, for we also arranged the arms in such a way. We returned the body back to the Earth, to the one who took it. With the funeral, some rest may come for the weary soul who was attached to the bones.

"Rest in peace, brother," Zeke spoke over the body. He built his marker, the Inukshuk, as the headstone for the grave. Then he turned to me. "You know I would go with you to the end. Should it come to this, I would die proud, because I spent my life with my brother. That means more to me than all the wealth in the free world. I wouldn't have my life any other way. I need you to know that."

"Nor would I," I hugged him. "I know I have doubted this whole journey, but I wouldn't change my decision, given another chance. *I* would rather die young and adventurous with you here than to have lived long and had no purpose in my life. I am glad I came with you. As much as I miss our brothers back at home, I would have missed you more had I stayed. I couldn't imagine what life would be like without the brother kings reining. You really woke up the giants in us, you know that? You made us our best selves."

"That means a lot to me," Zeke coughed. "Now, let's let the dead man rest," He trudged onward into the thicket.

Through the pines, I could see a change taking place on the Earth. Leaves just weren't as green as they used to be. Some would see this as the beauty of Autumn, leaves igniting on fire with brilliant crimson and ochre. The world was ready for its next chapter. It was ready to move on to the inevitable.

Under his red flannel, Zeke was wearing out, wearing thin. Only when we bathed in rivers did we see just how our ribs protruded from our flesh. We had no muscle left, just skin holding together lanky bones. There was no food left from what we had packed. It was always our safety net, but now we were utterly in the hands of the gods. The trees laughed at us with their wind, they roared knowing they would outlast us. The smallest of saplings would be more fit to live than us. We could be reaped by Mother Nature in a heartbeat.

"We're going to need to establish ourselves soon," Zeke turned over his shoulder to me. We camped in the same spot for a few nights here and there if we found food nearby, but for the most part, we traveled each day.

"Think so? We should be choosy on where we dig in."

"The sooner the better, Lane."

"I get that, but great kings need a great kingdom. We can't leave a legacy of living in peasant country. No sir! As kings we should have only the best kingdom in all the world," I put my arm around Zeke. "Silver rivers, crisp and full of fish. Lush red dirt, that holds the roots of only the mightiest trees!"

"Okay," Ezekiel hacked for a bit, then flashed a half smile.

"Are you doing okay?" My enthused face became wrinkled with concern.

"Yeah, why?"

"You've been coughing a lot recently. Being sick out here isn't like being sick at home."

"Which is why there's nothing we can do about it. I'll be okay," He pressed on, giving up another cough as he went.

Soon we came upon another lake, one of countless we've seen on our journey. The bay was covered though, hidden beneath stocks of wild rice.

"What do you know about agriculture?" Zeke asked me.

"Not enough," I knew he had the same idea that just crossed my mind. We took off our boots, rolled our jeans above our knees, and stepped into the water. I began breaking the heads off of the plants, storing them in a pouch that I made by folding my shirt up. Zeke had a different method, I noticed as I looked over at him. He ran his hand across the stock and kernels of rice fell out into his palm. He pocketed the fistful of rice and went back to shore to get the pot to collect them in. "You look like Huck Finn!" I called to him as he put of a stock of the wheat-like rice in his mouth.

"What month do you think it is?" Ezekiel asked, laying on his back and looking up at the full moon. We had been here a few days now, collecting as much rice as we could.

"Zeke, it's a harvest moon," I was in awe, having just realized the good omen we had been given.

We kept pushing north, finding more and more waterways in our path. Day and night, we trekked forward, pioneering into the frontier. The sun guided us, and the stars watched over us; singing lullabies as we slept around a fragile fire.

I began to recognize where I was; I knew the vastness and distinctness of the area. This region had rivers for veins, with ancient boulders for a spine, and the presence of God as the air of its lungs. Life here only existed in its most primal form, no acclimation to humanity. This biome was kept sheltered away, the sacred heart of the old Turtle Island.

Ten thousand years ago, glaciers filled this land. They made the Great Lakes and etched the rest of the ten thousand into Minnesota's surface. The glaciers uprooted stone as old as the Earth and left a scar of iron in the soil. As the glaciers receded into history, they made one final masterpiece: The Boundary Waters. This is where we found ourselves now.

"You were right," Zeke turned to me as we gazed at the view.

"About what?" I asked him.

"That a place like this is fitting to be called a kingdom," He began to walk along the shores of the endless lakes that rolled into each other. Islands stood tall from the icy waters with trees like mountains. This place was beautiful and yet gave a sense of resilience. There were ecosystems so fragile on Earth, they would wither at the first sign of mankind. Here, if anyone even muttered "humanity," a hundred thousand echoes would roar back. The voice in the wilderness would shout and its bestial spirit would not be tamed.

We stuck to the waterways as we looked for a place to settle. Fish were plentiful in these streams and in the murk of the lakes. Along the way we came across an inlet, where the water formed into a small pond and the land dipped down to meet it. Old pines cradled the little divot with branches interlocking like a fence. Without a word, we both set our stuff down and began to set up camp. Zeke dug a hole for a fire pit as I began chopping logs.

"Bring some long ones down to the water. We could make this pond into a fish trap," Zeke ordered. I nodded and did just that.

There were plenty of downed trees in the area, it just required a bit of searching. I don't think either of us were concerned with getting lost if we split from each other. We both had a keen sense of direction and natural awareness. Whether this was a God-given sixth-sense or something we learned through years of orienteering in the scouts, I cannot say.

I came back with more trees to cut up and Ezekiel was already down in the water, forming his trap. With the logs, he made a wall which directed the flow of water into the inlet. This carried in fish and kept them isolated in the pool. The project would take a few days for each of us to perfect. We had vertical posts that kept the logs from drifting away, this was reinforced with rocks and mud. We also made another wall to help prevent the incoming fish from getting out. Afternoons of work in the bitter water were followed with drying ourselves and our clothes over the fire.

"It's nice out here. Way out here," I sighed as the fire in the sky was burning out and the embers below us were growing hotter.

"Yeah? Why do you say that?"

"I feel like this is why we set out in the first place. *This* is the sort of home we were looking for. Not being on the move every day and just resting here, it feels like how I imagined it. We can really fortify ourselves here, build shelters and everything we need to really live here. Not just survive day by day."

"I see that now, I think drifting on the road so far has taken a lot out of me, but I know what you mean. Now that we're here, in our kingdom," He chuckled. "It feels like how I imagined it, too.

The Harbinger

Our fur was growing thick with each passing month. I had hardly noticed the indelicate goatee that grew in the place of my disciplined, shaven face. Zeke's hair was also getting longer, and more twigs stuck out from his curls like antlers. Even frequent bathes in the lake couldn't wash off all the dirt that was nestled in our skin. Nor could we keep up with the ticks that crept into our flesh. We were real woodsmen now. We were slowly losing ourselves to the elements of nature. Our humanity gave way to the spirits of wilder people. Soon enough, bark would replace our hide and we would become like walking trees. I was already waking up with fallen leaves on me.

We spent our days building and establishing ourselves in the nook of the world. Sturdy roofs were built over our grass beds. They were padded with moss and clay and had one wall that reached the ground. Our structures made a "V" with the fire pit in the middle and the walls facing outward. The mouth of the "V" faced the fish pool, which needed ongoing repairs and so far, had caught no fish.

Our huts resembled birds' nests, if we were to step back and see how little we and them had in difference.

Tirelessly we worked each day. We used the rope we had to tie up logs to create nearly every necessity. Traps were set, and tools were rigged, as if civilization had just been born. It looked as if we were the first men to become bipedal; as if fire was our own invention. Zeke made spears for fishing and in case we had to take up a more primal way of hunting.

Regardless of what the day presented for us, we always ended around the fire, theatrically telling stories like the scops of old. Often, we would draw up stories of constellations or recite the tales of Beowulf. Our dramatic retellings usually included some wooden props and costumes made of plants and fresh pelts. We took turns stomping around the campground as we told our fables around the fire.

I once figured we would turn to be as savage as animals, but what kept us on the thread of humanity was the songs and legends we told. We kept each other going this way. The fiery spirit in each of us shown like two pale stars in an endless, dark frontier. We were last remnants of the primitive faith; that was the voyager, the saunterer, the scout. *This* was the Scout Spirit. We were taught that being a good scout was about being shining citizens, a list of dos and don'ts, yet something about that molded lawful-good alignment didn't sit well with me. I felt the modern bureaucracy of the scouts undermined this spirit. The Scout Spirit was wanderlust, chaotic, and it was reverence toward nature. It was a freeing spirit, one not of laws, but of freedom. Whether this fire would propel us through the winter, I yet not know.

Splashing in the fishpond woke me one night. My eyes weren't yet adjusted to the dark, but I walked by ear to the pool where the fish trap was made. As my sight came to me, I began to see a boulder moving about. Its head came out from the murk and in its mouth was a fish. We were being robbed by a beaver. I reached back to the axe, keeping my eyes locked on the thief.

"Not tonight," I brought down the axe on its back. Again, I plunged the blade into the creature, who was now trying to get away. Robbing us was his last mistake.

The smell of smoked meat brought Zeke out of bed. I had already laid the skin out to dry and took the guts far off from camp. The rest of the rodent was roasting over the fire on a spike.

"Is it Thanksgiving already?" He mumbled as he was throwing on his jeans.

"Might as well be. This guy was the one tearing up our trap and stealing our fish. His death is as good as any reason to give thanks."

"Well, praise be to God," Zeke chuckled, squatting down beside me. We pulled meat off of the corpse, stretched sinew from the bone. Ezekiel almost spit out his food in laughter, when he noticed I had put the animal's head on a pike. "Camp Beaver Head!" He cheered and began to parade around. "Lest any animal walk in our dominion and not know. Despair creatures, savages of nature! Woe to the fiends of the Earth, woe to the flocks of the air, woe to all the beasts in the water! All paws who tread here shall know of our kingship; they shall fear the names of their kings!" He howled. Zeke began to dance around the fire. I sat amused, watching him howl and chant around the flames.

His wail cut bitterly to silence. The sudden stillness made my hair jump. Zeke's hands quivered almost as much as his mouth. Petrified myself, I moved only my eyes to see what Zeke had noticed. A wolf cloaked in scraggly grey fur, lean with ice in its eyes glared at us. The guts of the beaver hung from the bloodstained jaws. Cooked meat carries a heavy scent in the wilderness, I wasn't surprised he tracked it to us. I lunched for the axe.

"Back!" I waved the weapon. "Back!"

"You hear us? Get back you filthy mutt!" Zeke joined in. He reached for a burning branch that had been in the fire and whirled it in the air. The wolf kept its gaze as he backed into the brush, vanishing within the foliage.

"Dammit," I threw down the axe. "He'll be back and with others next time."

"There was nothing we could have done, Lane. You disposed of the guts. What else could we have done?"

"We might have passed unnoticed if you hadn't declared to the whole Northern hemisphere where we were hiding! I hope you got your point across, cause I don't think they know that they're supposed to be afraid of us. I think they know *we're* scared!" I shoved him.

"Hey! You think it's my fault? They could smell that meat cooking long before they heard me," I turned away from him. "It's no one's fault, we just got unlucky."

"Yeah, we got really fucking unlucky. Now they're going to come and slaughter us!"

"How do you know that?"

"They're wild animals. If they find food, they'll be back for more. It's not that complicated."

"Okay, well what do we do about it then? You want to pack up and find another camp? If they are coming back, they will just follow us to the next camp. Let's stay here, Lane. Build some defenses and traps, have a rotating watch, fortify ourselves until we know they've moved on."

"Alright," I gave up on being angry. "I'll start cutting wood. Go dig a mote around camp or something."

I drug the axe out into the forest. Chopping wood was the best therapy a man had out in the frontier. It was certainly calming to break things vigorously.

If adventure did call us, why would he betray us? Why would adventure tell us to go this route if he knew it would mean our own demise? I wrestled with the thought as I swung the axe around. We were driven out here and adventure decided we were not the champions he wanted, and now we were cut off and left to fend for ourselves. All the escapades we thought up as little boys never ended like this. We imagined conquering the wilds, one beast at a time. I walked into this forest with the notion that I was a lord of all. Now, I believe I am the least of these. We devoted our lives to the wild's call and now we would be repaid with toil. It would begin to rain on us with endless travail. The gods abandoned us. The gods of man lost to the gods of nature. They were killed and we were next.

I trudged back with the trees dragging behind me, hitched by the rope we had. Zeke had dug a trench around our nook with the shovel and exalted it with spikes. For time's sake, the wall around our camp would be an entanglement of fallen trees. Branches stacked on top of another, with sharpened spears made a *cheval de frise*, a "horse breaker," a line of anti-cavalry defense for us to hide behind. Ezekiel wasn't so confident in our construction, he said if a fox went up on the wall, it would break it down.

I planned to spend following days getting the adequate wood to build a Lincoln Log style wall, but for tonight the mess of pine branches would have to do. We cornered ourselves against the water, creating a semi-circle of spikes and barriers. All we could do is hunker down and prepare for siege behind the barricade. The beaver head was moved so it could be seen far from over the wall. It was our war flag, a red banner of our kingdom. Though, if I were to vulnerably honest, neither of us wholeheartedly believed in our royalty anymore.

We spent that night with our backs against the water and the fire between us and the abyss of a forest ahead. I understood how the pilgrims conceived the idea that the forest was evil. It was lovely on the surface, but its soul was more twisted, untamed. Any red spirit of courage we had could be snuffed out.

"I saw a jackalope today," Zeke said nonchalantly out of the silence.

"What?" I had zoned out and was completely caught off guard by his comment.

"I saw a jackalope. Just right over there."

"No, you didn't," I scoffed.

"Yeah, I did. He came hopping out of the bush just right there, in between those two thickets."

"Bullshit," I laughed. "You sure you didn't just see a rabbit?"

"Yes, it had the antlers and everything. I'm not making this up!"

"Alright, Zeke. I mean, I could believe you saw a *doe* jackalope. You know? No antlers."

"So basically, a rabbit?"

"Yeah, I would believe you saw a rabbit," He shook his head. We sat in stillness for a moment, just staring into the fire.

"I miss home, Lane," Zeke turned our conversation.

"Where did that come from?"

"I'm scared. I can't even sleep through the night, because there would be nothing I could do to defend myself. The savages could come and devour us, and we couldn't do a thing about it. The powers that be wouldn't intervene, they would leave us to die out here," He lamented.

"Then we don't sleep. We've gone without sleep before. For what it's worth, I miss home too. But we can't rest in that now. We can't move forward from clinging to the past. You need to let things pass, look to where you are *now*. You were once very caught up in the future, so you took every risk you could to make it happen. Yet, now that you're standing in it, you realize how much you left. There are repercussions to leaving your home and family. That's been the promise from the beginning. You took adventure with the tip of a sword, and you got yourself cut."

"I don't regret our decision," He told me plainly. "Yes, I am afraid. And yes, it is hard to leave home, but I'm not giving up our crusade."

"Good. Cause then I would have put twenty-five years of faith into the wrong person," I throw him the words he told me so long ago. "I would brave hell or high water for you. I would brave it all because I know you wouldn't quit on me."

"I'm not quitting on you, Lane."

"Not now, but in case you start to. I know you look back when you walk."

Despite our vows, we passed out not long after. The beaver's head would have to keep watch in our absence. Sleeping with the axe wouldn't save me now.

Twigs crippling brought me up to the surface of sleep, but I wasn't as alert as I should have been. The beaver had no way of telling us. As Ezekiel woke up, he did not see the green trees, nor the smoldering logs. He saw only grey tangled fur, hanging over him.

"Fuck," He shot back. "Lane get up!" Zeke screamed as he tried to get to his feet. The hound drooled over him. Paws pushed against the Earth, as the feral wolf lunged at Ezekiel. The wolf bit down on his arm, which Zeke brought up to defend himself. He cried in anguish. Before the beast could rip off Zeke's limb, I split into its ribs with the axe. Ezekiel found the shovel and also brought that down on the wolf. It yelped, but never took his fury off of us. We chanted at the dog, swinging our weapons at him.

"Zeke, there's more!" The pack was panting at us from across our wall, trying to figure out how to cross over the trees. We backed to the water's edge as more wolves tried to make the jump over the mote.

"Swim!" Zeke turned and leapt into the river.

I did the same. I didn't even look where I was treading, but I was going full bore. The icy water clashed against my face and chilled my soul to the core. I couldn't tell if it was the barking or splashing of water, but it was the only thing I could hear. Not even my rhythmic breaths made a sound to me. All my faith was placed in Zeke's assumption that wolves wouldn't follow us into the water. He proved to be right. Though their lack of pursuit wasn't due to their inability to follow us.

As I waded in the water, I saw the pack run off. Perhaps they were discouraged by one of their own being injured. Zeke was nearly across the flowing lake by now. I kept myself afloat for a while, just to catch my breath before swimming back to shore.

"We're gonna play a game," The little boy called as he dug a box out from the piles of stuff his living room collected.

"What kind of game?" I asked Zeke. It was the first time I had ever been to his house. The memory was so long ago, I forgot there was ever a time when he and I weren't friends.

"An adventure game. We pretend to be heroes and we slay dragons and kill giants," He unfolded a map, beautifully detailed and colored. I didn't care to ask if this place was real or not. "Here,

this one's yours," As he placed figurines around the table, he handed me one. The tiny man was crudely painted and wielded an axe. "It's a barbarian. A fighter, just like you," I smirked.

I tore down what we had set up of camp, throwing all of our equipment into the pack. It nearly took a spyglass to find Zeke huddled on the other bank. I swam back to where Zeke was sitting on the shore. All our stuff curled with me, weighing me down, sometimes pulling me beneath the surface. I found him clenching his left arm and tears leaving his eyes. His face was white and dying.

I hurled the bag down on the banks and dug for the first-aid kit. A wad of disinfectants and athletic wrap was brought out from the metal box. Zeke didn't respond to this, nor when I removed his coat. The stinging of the alcohol made him wince back into life. I wiped the blood and water from him torn forearm, then wrapped it tightly with the tape. I took my own tee shirt from under my layers and tore it and wrapped it around Ezekiel's left arm as a sling.

"Thanks," He murmured.

Clairvoyant

The War of Attrition

From the infinite waterways and rushing lakes, rose an island, like Excalibur being presented to us. This island would serve as our saving fortress in a war we were now fighting, our secret nation, our Avalon. A place for kings to seek respite and regain their strength.

It was modest in size, but lush with evergreens and plant-folk, all sharing their nutrients through the web of deep roots. We found the place after a few days on the run; portaging across rivers and hiking through groves. For the first nights at our new home, we had two camps set up. Zeke stayed on the island, digging in, while I slept across the bank. We both knew resources on the island were limited, so I explored the mainland and gathered what I could find.

Near the center of the island was the largest of pines, whose roots were exposed by a divot in the ground. Ezekiel took the natural cradle and built our shelter there. The roof just inched above the ground, laying logs across the hole and digging further into the heart of the island. He padded the top with the usual moss and clay, insulating the years remaining heat. All of which was impressive to do with only one functioning arm.

While he did this, I was busy cutting and stacking logs on the shore. I also spent the nights sharpening a host of spikes. The island in of itself was difficult to get upon, but a few added protective measures couldn't hurt. From what I could see from my fire to his, Zeke was clearing brush from the core of the island and pushing everything outward. The spikes would then be hidden among the tangled mess of vines and branches. Not even a bull moose would be able to tread onto our land.

Most of those nights were spent pondering how safe we would be on the island. We both agreed on the location. However, him and I were both aware that wolves could swim, should they want to come after us. Right now, it was difficult to go from the thigh-deep water to the top of the island's ledge, but once winter rolls around, the wolves would have no issue getting to us from the ice.

It was eerily lonesome being across the water from Ezekiel those nights. We could see the light from each of our fires, but still I felt alone in the world. The breath of relief from getting personal time didn't outweigh the dependency that had grown between us.

He worried me. His clay mask was breaking under everything recently and now he probably feels exiled to his own little country. I know he hoped bitterly that the glory of our kingdom returned. I wanted it too more than anything, to see our fiery sprit restored, but I don't blame anything that doubted us.

"Ahoy!" Zeke called from the banks as I swam the lumber over to him. He stood like a proud captain of his ship. "What news of the new world?"

"The Corps of Discovery has found many great resources; we bring back furs and lumber!" I played along, tossing my bundles onto the shore.

"Aye," Zeke hoisted me out of the sea. "Avalon is already flourishing with trade," He showed me the lodge he had built into the ground.

"Alas, I am liking the new world!" I gave out in a heavy accent. We stood in contentment over our island for a moment. "How are you?" I asked sincerely.

"Uh, I'm good," Zeke scratched his shaggy head with his only hand left.

"Yeah? Your arm doing okay?"

"Yeah, Lane. I'm alright," He laughed and shook his head.

"That's good to hear. Well, hey, I'm going to swim over the rest of our supplies, so I'll be back," I dove into the merciless water and in a few dozen strokes, I was across the river. The air was getting crisp and it was warmer to keep my clothes on when in the water. As long as I could dry them quickly after getting to shore. I kept a spare change of clothes at camp to change into quickly, to help reheat my body from the unforgiving river.

The hole in the ground that Zeke dug wasn't too bad considering we were sleeping with worms. Once we finish the barricade along the island's rim, Zeke and I talked about furnishing the inside with logs. Potentially even trying to fire clay to make bricks. We knew this would have to be our stronghold for the foreseeable future, so for the first time, we started to plan past our noses.

Auras of heat irradiated from the fire that evening. My outer clothes still drip-drying around the flames. We were reminiscing our days in the scouts again. Talking about legendary tales that seemed like a whole lifetime ago. I had once pretended to be a bear outside of Riley's tent. I snorted and pawed at the young boy inside, only to be met with a frying pan, like a Louisville Slugger, to the face. There was even talk that long ago, the older boys picked up a scout's tent while they were sleeping and brought it down to the lake. The poor guy floated off and had to paddle his way back to shore on his air-mattress.

Our conversation was halted with a noise competing over the fire's. Marching. The sound of a million marching. Like a battalion coming down on us. Louder it grew, more men marching. Zeke ran outside to see what was going on. He couldn't see it, not at first.

"What do ya see?" I called from my lounging.

Deep within the boreal forest, came the storm. A wall of rain stampeding across the lakes with enough water to flood the observable world. Sooner than he could yell "rain," Zeke was drenched. He darted back inside, but not even our hut was safe. Water came in from every porous structure we made. Steam replaced our fire, night then replaced day. Our sleeping bags and all of our clothes were all soaking up every ounce of water that intruded our home. With our light gone, we couldn't see any of our gear to make improvements. Nothing we could do to save our sinking ship. At a certain point, we had to bite the bullet and just sleep in the bog that was our house.

"Huh, now we know what that scout felt like when his tent was thrown into the lake," I managed to hear Ezekiel say through the roar of the storm. We had experienced rain earlier in our journey, all mild and gentle to us. This was another nature; this rain came from different heavens. It was angry and wrathful. A foreign oppressor we could not outmatch.

I woke up the next morning from a frog mistaking my face for a lily pad. It appeared our lodge was still flooded, for the rain hadn't stopped. Mud was growing onto my sleeping bag and it seemed that already fish could start inhabiting our home.

"Zeke, how long has it been since we've last eaten?" I asked, running out of rice long before we got to the island.

"I can tell you how long it's been since our last bath," He shot back, in annoyance with the brown water.

"See what you can do around here, I'm going to find some food."

"Okay," He laid his mop of a head back down into the pond, assumingly back to sleep.

I plunged my legs in the water and began to circumvent the island. No crawfish, nor turtle, nor even a leech could be found. I swam over to the mainland. Nothing in God's creation was present. There were no berries, not even the ones that shouldn't be consumed. I heard no squirrels, no loons. There was absolutely nothing. Every living thing had left the world.

"What the hell?"

I really wished the druid in me would kick in; that some divine spark would bring back what I learned in grade school Ecology. Yet nothing came. I wish I knew the names of every tree and could point out which parts of each plant is edible, but I couldn't. I was so heavily dependent on animals being available to slaughter. We had grown lazy in searching for food, now we would suffer for it. We were craftsmen of fire; that was a power we had harnessed since our youth. We were the gods of flint and steel, devoting ourselves to destruction. The very courage in our souls was a blazing red. It was the element of strength and rage, but we didn't take the time to learn the art of eating the land. How foolish we were as boys to focus on the things of the world that can destroy rather than restore.

When I returned to the island, I could see now just how much the rain had depressed the roof of our hut. Even though the drizzling had frozen, the world was still dripping from its resounding effects.

Though, Zeke was able to bounce back from what was lost in last night's flood. He dug a trench around the outer brim of the hut and refortified the back wall, where the roots grow. He was planning on tackling the roof as well but knew he would have to tear it all off in order to make any substantial enhancements.

"I'll have to use some of the wood you brought over," He gathered. "Adding cross beams will only make the ceiling more durable and keep in more heat."

"Yeah, go for it," I shivered, rubbing my hands together. I knew this needed to be a priority over making fences. What good is building up ramparts if there's no castle to defend? I helped him peel back the clay and moss from the existing A-frame structure. "You know, we could utilize the stones we have around here, make some nice walls." Since all we had so far was the dirt box Zeke shaped out.

"Or make bricks," Zeke pointed back to his original idea.

"I think rocks may need to suffice for now. We can definitely patch them with clay and try to harden it with torches."

"Okay, I guess we could do that," It seemed the rain had drenched us to our soul and damped our spirits further.

I will admit, even though my work for the fence was undone, the new roof was looking pretty solid. An added layer goes a long way in shelter building. We also built little, elevated beds out of several layers of lined-up branches and ferns. Somewhere along the line we heard that the key to survival is getting off the ground. Probably was one of the only things we *did* learn from Wilderness Survival merit badge.

"You know what sounds really good right now?" Zeke said aloud, while lying down.

"What?"

"Pine tea. We have everything we need right on the island."

"That's true. Wanna brew some?"

"Yup," he hulled himself out of his damp sleeping bag. I gathered up some wood to resurrect the fire and went down to the shore to fill the pot with water. Pine tea was a simple elixir to make. Take pine needles. Boil.

We even added some sap to act as honey, we didn't dare go looking for a beehive to scavenge. Despite being a crude drink, we actually didn't mind the taste. The scent of fresh-cut pine filled our log cabin and roasted our lungs. Our mouths tasted like Yuletide. The drink heated us from the inside outward and made sitting on the waterlogged, dirt ground much more bearable.

"We should really start to spice this place up," The novelty of drinking tea was sinking in. "Nice hardwood floors, mahogany furniture, and a great hearth right on the back wall."

"And bricks," Zeke added.

"Oh yeah! Huge brick chimney and a nice set of stairs going up to the surface. Shingled roof and insulated walls. Hell, we could get running water in here!"

I could tell that my friend's spirits were lifted slightly, with the smirk on his face. But there was no denying that he was slipping into a deeply rooted depression. The air was getting colder, and the nights were growing darker. As we walked from the bright days of summer into the inevitable winter, he grew more and more reluctant to keep marching.

We still had daylight in our hands. I told Zeke to rest up as I got started to gather materials for our home, seeing it as the only way to lift ourselves up. Walking around the island, I started by hoisting large rocks out from the water. I still looked for any fish-life that could have been lurking on our shores, but still there were none.

Then, I went around from where I left the rocks to bring them back to our site. For a moment, our island was the host of a *cromlech*, a circle of archaic standing stones. Our hut was in the center. I almost felt guilty for defiling the shrines, which I had happened into existence not a few hours earlier. Piling the stones in front of the house in the hole, I noticed no sign of Ezekiel. From behind my mouth was covered. My knees were knocked forward, forcing me to the ground.

"Look," A whisper entered my ear. His breath could be seen through the dew. Between the weeds and water, I saw it drift by.

Polished oak, hand-carved and waxed so bright. The craft made no sound as it drifted along the river. The man in the canoe also had his gazed fixed in our direction. His paddle was like a feather to the water, making absolutely no sound, and only perpetuating the park ranger ever so slightly forward. He was husky, burly auburn beard, and a uniform as clean as a whistle. It resembled our scout get-up. More accurately, our uniforms resembled his. If it weren't for Zeke, I think I would have forgotten what a human looked like. The man and his canoe glided passed us and then went on their way.

"Damn, that was close."

"We should really be careful," Zeke pushed himself off of me. "We're clearly not alone out here."

I went back to gathering the rocks, naming them according to where they would fit in the house. Zeke had started to pile more clay for us to use as mortar in between the mason work. The rocks didn't stack nice, even after I went through each one to see which piece would fit the best. I was really hoping the clay would hold up, especially after Zeke took a torch to it; trying to solidify the wall.

We were only able to build half of a wall with the stones I gathered. I dreaded going out for more. The icy waters were getting less and less tolerable. It took longer to recover and bring myself back to warmth with each dive. But we thought it valuable enough to fortify the house. Keeping the heat in during winter would be life or death.

As I yet again, plunged into the rains of the earth, I wondered about all the struggle to come. We still haven't any food. We needed to start utilizing the river or hunting again, because pine tea could only do so much for us. We had a white flag float past us today, we could have thrown in the towel, given in and gone home. All at the reward of eating again, but we didn't. We consciously chose to stay in the fight.

I was so hungry those days, my stomach physically felt as if it were being wrung out. The steady lifting of rocks and hand work kept my mind off the thought of starving, but at night in the stillness, that's when it was most painful. We started eating the bark and chewing the sap of the trees on the island. The tree mocked us for our suffering. They spat at us, the ferns and weeds too, all the flora watched in anticipation for our demise. I wouldn't be long.

Night had just overtaken the day when Zeke and I were brewing more tea. The fire shown bright against the cast iron pot. Steam from our cups and vapor from our breaths filled the lodge with a warm mist. A ghostly howl came roaring into the land, nearly putting the fire out. I had forgotten what we were laughing about, we were so shook.

I climbed outside and pulled the axe from the stone earth. Snow had begun to cover it, as I noticed after gripping the cold timber handle. Zeke ascended right behind me.

"There he is," Ezekiel pointed out the wolf that gave out another monstrous howl. He was lean, starvation was getting to him too. His ribs protruded from his fur and his tongue lay dry from his fangs. It seemed we were both competing for the same food source. This band of wolves was, however, outstandingly fiercer in their search for food. A few other savages ran past him, yelping out war cries. The chief, the alpha, not long after began to run behind the pack, but not before shooting us with a glare.

"If nothing else, you," The timber wolf called out. We were marked men. The phantoms vanished into the brush, which was painted white now, as the rain froze. We must've been working in the house and looking down in the dirt so long that we hadn't noticed the snow starting to accumulate. The top layers of the world were powdered in the frozen grey.

"We need to be more active in stocking up for winter," I laid out the obvious.

"Haven't we been? You said you couldn't find any signs of animal life. You saw the wolves just as I did, they're starving and they're in panic about it. The only thing they can do is pursue the hunt. What happens when there is no prey for them? They'll just keep running."

"No, they'll come for us. I believe that, they have the ability and the intent. They're waiting."

"For what?" Zeke waved from across the fire that night, also gesturing with his sling.

"The ice. They can't get onto the island from the water, but when the lake freezes over, they'll be on us. There won't be a warning, either. They'll be on us in the dead of night when that damned water first freezes and then we're done."

"No. If they are waiting for the ice, we can prepare for that. We can wall the island."

"What good would that do? The snow would cover it all and make a ramp straight to us. We could barricade ourselves in this hole and they would dig us up."

"So, do we just let them win, just let it happen?"

"No."

"Then what, Lane?!" Zeke stood, throwing down his cup of water. "You're gonna say we get them first? Come on, we injured one wolf by chance, there is no way in hell you could take on a whole pack on your own and even hope to live. You would be torn apart!"

"We won't stand an assault. There is nothing we can build that they can't destroy. We need to be actively undermining their source of food, because they have to have something right now. And then we need to be ready take them on. We need to be on the offensive, we cannot wait for them to starve off on their own."

"This is suicide, Lane," He sat back down on the log stool. "'Undermine their food source?' Come on, how are you gonna do that? I don't see how you could ever do that. We can't leave the island. If they *are* waiting for us, leaving the island is their invitation to kill us."

"So, we're trapped?" I pondered for a heartbeat. "No, leaving the island is our best bet. I'm willing to swim in that water if it means getting food for us and taking food from them. You can do things around the island to help fortify the place but sitting in this hole can't be our only strategy."

"Okay."

Days came and went. I took regular swims in the lake to search for life, while Zeke made reinforcements to our tiny country. He cut down branches and replaced the spikes that were used to rebuild the roof.

I traveled along the river, as a natural guide. Each day I would press further down than I did before. I wasn't so brave as to scout downstream overnight. I needed the security that came with being by my brother. Each day grow colder and darker. As I wanted to stretch how far I could travel, the night pushed back and stretched how far its darkness could reign over the world.

Deep green cloaked in ice was the forest I lived in. I spent so much of my time being consumed by the pressure and anxiety of what was to come, that I often forgot the beauty that drove me out into the world. Here, was a place of ancient life, full and strong.

Then, I came across a scar in the Earth; a sliver of dead trees. No green left to boast of the Ent's former glory. The bones of the trees were white, not with snow, but as if every living cell and soul were expelled. All the trees had fallen. No, they had been struck down. Each had been hand-picked for judgement.

Not far off from the valley of dead trees, was the evil soul who reaped them.

"Something had to die for me to gain," They thought. A beaver had taken the beauty of the unadulterated forest and corrupted it. It twisted her branches in ways that didn't belong. The hag weaved the dead bodies of her slain together to form her lodge. Spikes and barbs clawed out of the shell of her house. Only from recognizing the beauty of the world, did I see the corruption.

Home or not, I would bring my judgement down onto their house. She could not craft a spell nor hex to save herself. I swung the axe. Again, and again, I brought down the blade on the lodge. Branches snapped, and chips flew every way that they could. The heat from the activity began to warm my clothes, still damp after wading in the lake.

Not long after my attack, hissing came from the cavern. I couldn't see the fiend, but I felt it clawing at my axe with each swing. The roof began to cave in on the beaver. It could have dived into the water and escaped under the thin ice, but she didn't. She stayed to fight and scratch at me.

Once I did spot the witch, I took my focus off of her house and went straight for her. Another kill could carry us enough to hunt and kill again. If the hag's face wasn't wretched enough, it certainly was after one well-placed strike. I beheaded the animal just to make sure it was dead, before dragging it back to camp. The only thing more satisfying than burning the witch, was being able to eat. That supper was the greatest feast we had thus far. The hot meal fueled our souls to carry on.

Ice was rapidly tainting the water; leaking from the shores and slowly infecting the deeper rifts. I found signs on my travels, of the wolves beginning to test the new ground. They were practicing for us. They only thing good about the lake freezing over, was the shortening of my swim. The water got more unbearable with each dip, taking longer to get myself warm. I always started out running to help fight the process of frost bite. It was haunting to think that the water in my skin and in my blood froze, making the crystal shards cut my flesh from within. The stiffer my hands were, the more internal ice had to be shattered with every move.

I found footprints in the fresh layers of snow. I traced their paws, which were not so different from my own, up to the north bank of the river. The heat from their pads melted the snow to create the illusion that their paws were bigger than in reality. Yet, I fell for their trick and believed myself to be tracking giants. Further and further into the evening, I followed the trail. A few acres and a few hours deeper into the night, I followed the monsters. Panting with adrenaline, my breath was blurring my vision. Then, the footprints vanished. As if the wolves, all in one bound, leaped far into the mountains.

"Where are you?" I panicked. I furiously turned about, expecting them to flank me in the moment. "Where are you?!" I screamed with a voice that matched the thunder. Another voice came from the grey wind, echoing with the same power.

On the other side of the lake, they revealed themselves to me. Wolves or so I recognized them. There was no distinction between man and beast at this point. Had they been indigenous savages wearing the coats of timber wolves, I would have not noticed a difference. They danced and barked, celebrating their hunt.

I exchanged glares with their chief. He flashed his fangs, as did I, tightening my grip on the axe. The raid darted off, back into the haze grey. I started to run. I fled back along the shore to our camp. Darkness set in too soon. While I had tracked the predators, I had forgotten to track to the sun. How the evil spirits were laughing at me now.

I heard barks and howls from behind me. No way I could outrun them and if they swam over to me, swimming away also wouldn't save me. I had to face them. I had meet them head on and give them hell. Sliding to a stop on the ice, I turned around. The one, the chief was the only wolf pursuing me. The champion of the animal kingdom was sent out to fight. He struggled to keep traction out on the ice and slowed his pace to a halt. Our eyes locked, glaring each other down. We huffed clouds of vapor into the arctic air.

"Come on!" I yelled at the beast. I struck the ice with the axe handle, egging him on. I met the unyielding carnage in his eyes. He snarled as he pawed the snow, running toward me. Clawing the ground back with each stride, splinters of ice shot up in his wake. I dug in my heels in and prepared to clash with the feral god of bloodlust. The very breath of this beast was stained in death.

I swung my weapon, throwing myself off balance as he passed. As I turned to meet him, I saw that I had clocked his snout. He scrambled to stop momentum from sliding further than he wanted. Without sparing a moment, he charged again. His weight blew past my axe, not having enough time to prepare a full swing. He came back to strike me in the leg. I twisted out as he tugged, to see he still had my calf in his mouth.

"Fuck!" I screamed. From my back, I swung at him. Relentless sweeping of the axe kept him on guard. I pushed myself to my knees and struck the dog in the skull. He yelped and dropped the meat from his jaws. Again, I slashed at its face with the axe, forcing myself to a stand. Straight down on the spine, I struck. The wolf, more and more immobile. I fell on top of its crooked back, losing my strength. I wrapped my arms around its neck and squeezed in. The dog got its second wind of fighting spirit, but it wasn't enough. I clenched the damn wolf with every ounce of what men might call "strength."

"That's right!" It fell limp in my arms. I kicked it once I brought myself to my feet. I ripped off my coat and used my undershirt as a tourniquet. "Dammit," I spat as I cinched down with the blood-soaked shirt. I threw on the coat and began to hobble toward the island. I had no idea how far it was, only by the mercy of the stars was I even able to see. "Zeke!" I hollered into the abyss. "Zeke!" My steps misplaced themselves more frequently. The axe made for a cane as I limped, leaving a trail of blood in the snow.

My vision came and went. I felt my legs move, but I could not tell if I was even moving. My eyes closed to reveal a subtle darkness. I opened my eyes to see the stars. They were gorgeous. I had never seen them so clear in all my life. They blended gracefully into the snow that descended to earth and began to cover my body.

I once thought that we would resort back to our primal ways. That we would turn to animals. In death, I know this wasn't true. An old bear will isolate himself, trekking miles to seek desolation, so that none may see him weak. A warrior bear would rather be slaughtered in battle than to wither away. Never more in my life have I felt the need for another human being. In this moment I didn't want to be without Ezekiel. This bear needed his friend.

"Stop!" Zeke coughed. "Get off! Stop it!" The little boy had been pinned down by bullies on the playground. They punched him, for what was no good reason, other than to simply hurt something.

"Get off!" I shoved the one kid who was on top and swung at the other. The attacker looked up in horror from his bloody nose, now dripping into the concrete. The two kids ran off, crying to their teacher.

"Thanks," I pulled the tiny kid up from where he was. "Name's Zeke," He smiled through his bruised face and long, messy hair.

"Lane," I shook his hand.

I woke up again in the home. My brother holding me by the fire. The axe was leaned up in the corner. On top of the steps, I could see Zeke had made a small stone man, marking a chapter in our journey. "Please don't leave me. Lane, please don't give up," He cried, rocking my body with his. The fire couldn't even stop his cold tears from freezing. More than just my blood left me. My soul was also lost out in the snow fields. No song nor tales of yore could save me now.

Of everything in the world, I could have thought about, *Where the Wild Things Are*, was what came to mind. The creatures begged the boy not to leave in the end, saying they would eat him whole. I never understood that line until right now. They weren't threatening him. No, they would have rather resorted to cannibalism than to have their beloved king leave them. They would have eaten him if it meant he would still be with them.

"I'm sorry," He cried.

Clairvoyant

Christmas

He sat down at his desk and began to type out:

December 26, 1980,

A month back, reports came in about supposed "illegal campers," in the Pine Lake area, near the Border. Several unauthorized fire pits have also been found in the surrounding region. I paddled around the entire lake, but no sign of them had ever been found.

Two days ago, now, I went back up to Pine Lake to follow up on yet more reports. This time, claims came in about seeing fires at night and hearing yelling.

On Christmas day, I found two young men in a snowbank. Wolves had gotten to them. A mile trail of blood led me to the cave they were in. One of them was still alive, frost-bitten and hardly conscious. The other had died of major blood loss, due to a wolf bite to the right calf.

As of now, there is no way for me to get in contact of the authorities until I get back to the Gunflint Ranger Station.

The living one is resting yet, but the other is wrapped up and outside on the sled. Tomorrow at sunup, when it ain't deathly cold, I'll drive back down to the park station and get the situation handed over to the police.

As of now, this is the acting incident report until the authorities take over.

Denis Miller,

Park Ranger.

The funeral was respectable in size. All of the young men from the old gang gathered in their black ties and jackets. Allan and Jack talked quietly to each other. Rick was recently back in town after being medically discharged from the war. He stood in the back with a cigarette to calm his shivering composure, a habit he had certainly picked up from the Marines. Joe and his family were there, they mingled casually with the other parents. The only person not present was Ezekiel. He was in the passenger seat of a car, still parked on the slopes outside the cemetery. It was hard to tell who was more alone that day, him or my parents. None of the other adults ever knew my folks and now wasn't exactly the time to break the ice.

"I did this," Zeke said to himself, keeping his soft gaze on the cityscape below. The air was cold and still, not even the highway under his feet made a comprehensible sound. Only a knock on the window would take him away from wherever his mind held him. Zeke shook in terror as he slowly opened the car door.

"You're going to come out here and you're going to be there for him," The stern voice was my father. He gripped Ezekiel by the arm, the one with a sturdy plaster cast, and walked him up to the front of the crowd. My father had Zeke stand right next to him as they put my body into the ground. As they did, my brother fell to the dirt and began to weep. My dad with a stiff lip, had all the reason in the world to hate Ezekiel for getting me killed, but he let the boy cry uncontrollably over his feet.

Clairvoyant

Book Three
Redemption

Clairvoyant

Ghost Tales

Artic winters were one of the many known killers in the myths of men. Wind cut at the face like shards of glass, whipping relentlessly, scarring the flesh of everything present. Not even the ground was safe, the permafrost turned the lush soil into bitter rock with jagged crystals of ice, cutting at the animals that burrowed below.

Way out in the haze of a blizzard, a line of heavily coated men trudged through the frozen moonscape on snowmobiles. Their bones were under the grip of winter had no choice but to carry themselves further into the tundra. As night fell on them, in the distance, their target was in sight. Light. A fiery aura illuminated the fog of the snowstorm. Had they been through these parts in the white of the day, they would have ridden past the village, unknowingly.

The next morning was dead with several more feet of snow and a new canvas building in the road. One of the elders approached the shelter, as men were already outside tending their tent.

"*Ullaakuut*," He greeted good morning, handing one of the workers a cup of coffee.

"Cheers," The old man, worn with the hardships of age, went back to his house to bring out more coffee for the workers. Another Inuit came out to the base and listened in to the crew's conversations.

"English?" He piped up eventually. Getting the attention of the men. "You men speak English?"

"Aye," A black haired man in a wool-lined, cardinal, coat stepped out from the others. "We didn't expect anyone here spoke English."

"Some," The man modestly admitted. "You are not the only quallunaat we have seen. One lived with us for a few years, very recently."

"I didn't mean to assume. We just didn't expect for a village so far north, that you would have a lot of interaction with the white man." The Inuit scoffed. "I'm Captain Aedan Evans. We're with the Royal Geographical Society, here to explore and film the great arctic," Aedan gestured toward the horizon.

"Are you really exploring if you are clinging onto civilization?" The native man turned to look at his dingy town.

"You seem to know more than a little English," Aedan nervously chuckled.

"Only what the *white man* taught me," The old Inuit smirked.

"Yeah, I want to know about this man who's come through."

Inside the old man's house, the two sat down across from one another with a hot drink. Aedan, despite being experienced in years, would never be used to the fierce cold that the Inuits had nestled into for centuries.

"This man who was here, he taught you English?"

"Yes. He taught me English and we taught him Inuktitut. He lived with us for only awhile before he packed and left again. He showed up as you did: in the night, in a blizzard. I don't know what drove him out here, but he was, uh, determined on traveling further. It wasn't hard for us to figure him out, though."

"Well who was he?"

"We never learned his name, he never said it. We took to calling him *Tiguaak*, the adopted one. He was a nomad like our people were. He must have come from afar and I imagine he will walk much further before his legs stop."

"How long was he in the village?"

"A year or two, I'd say. He found us and wanted to learn as much as he could. We taught him how to hunt and fish, how to speak the language. He was in love with our culture, but no one was surprised when he left."

"Why would he leave?"

"Tiguaak heard of a myth, about a whole village disappearing overnight. No signs of anyone leaving, no signs of any bodies left behind, the people just vanished. But this was a generation ago."

"He left everything here to follow a bloody ghost story," He shook his head. "Why would he trek across the arctic alone for that?"

"He knows a truth that you may not yet."

"I'm not interested in your old-man wisdom," Aedan leaned forward, unimpressed. "I have enough experience under my belt."

"Of course," The elder looked out to the RGS explorers outside, still hooking up satellites and other commodities to their operations tent. "Now, we never said you could stay here," Aedan raised his brow. "You will be asked to leave, but we can't tell you which direction to go. You could hike back to society, to your comforts. *Or* you could follow this man; he could probably show you a thing or two. Who knows, maybe you will explore something that hasn't already been discovered? You want to film the arctic? Perhaps finding him would make for an excellent film."

Aedan stormed out of the house, hot in his own embarrassed rage.

"Take it down," He shouted, waving his arms at their tent. "Take it down!" His men looked confused.

"We just put the whole thing up," His men retaliated.

"Then you should bloody remember how to take it down," He spat at his crew member. "We're leaving!" Aedan and his men began ripping their base down and packing it back onto the wooden sleds they pulled it in. The elder and a few other villagers watched from their porch.

"Which way did he go? This *white man* which way did he go?" Aedan demanded the townsfolk who gathered to watch his mania. The natives pointed away from the sun, past a stone man that was hand built on the north edge of the village. "North it is."

Captain Aedan led his team back along the Innuksuak River, toward their basecamp. The Royal Geographical Society was working out of Inukjuak, Quebec. Their camp overlooked the Hudson Bay, which roared against the frigid seaside of the fishing village.

"Cikuq! Hey, make sure those cameras are ready in the morning," Aedan called to some of his men as he searched the building. "Cikuq! Where the hell is that eskimo?" The other crew members who were stationed there shrugged. Aedan ran upstairs to the map room and lookout tower. "Cikuq, I've only called your name fifty times."

"Welcome back, Captain Evans," The young native Inuit looked up from his charts.

"Save it. I need you to be our guide in this next expedition," Aedan shot quickly.

"Yeah, that's why you hired me as head of navigation," Cikuq didn't see Aedan's heated face from over his maps, which he had scatted across the room. The captain took a deep breath.

"I need you to come with us as a field guide," Aedan spoke slowly, continuing to breathe deeply.

"What's the occasion?"

"Have you ever heard of a story about a whole village disappearing up North?"

"Uh, yeah," Cikuq readjusted his round glasses and sat back in his seat. "It's up by Greenland, along the shore there."

"We're going to find it. More specifically, we're looking for a man who's probably in the village."

"Friend of yours?" He sarcastically asked.

"Not exactly. He apparently lived with the locals here for a few years then went to find this village on foot, that's all we know about him. The eskimos seemed to think pretty highly of him. So, we're going to make a special trip to go and see just how great he really is." Aedan started down the stairs. "We leave first thing tomorrow!"

The sun rose in the direction of southeast and would fall in the southwest, bringing only a few hours of daylight. A rusted orange Sno-Cat roared through the morning, pulling itself on tank tracks over the frozen ground. They crawled north, along the bay. Eventually, they caught the ferry across the Hudson Strait. The icy sea was home to huge swells of dark waves, which lightly tossed the ship as they went. Saltwater sprayed up at the men, who were on the deck, stretching their legs. The team's cameraman was fumbling over the pitch and roll of the boat to set up his tripod. He was eager to get as much film as possible for their documentary. Aedan found it all annoying and treated the video project as secondary to "his" explorations. He had been to South America, parts of Asia, and Africa. Even after going across the world, the man never seemed content with his achievements. He'd be damned if he found someone who'd travelled more than him.

"Frobisher Bay," Aedan read the sign for the town they landed in, which was in English, French, and Inuktitut glyphics. The fishing village held little more than few thousand and was where the team would rest for the night. After only a few hours of sleep and planning, the team refueled the truck and left.

They passed tirelessly through the snow. The null of the engine disrupted centuries of lifeless silence. When the sun did rise, it revealed how little there was in the world. Mile after mile, they journeyed over the frost. Salt and ivory seemed to cover the immense world in front of them. Cikuq was diligent to mark the maps with the coordinates of each landmark they passed. With each point, he steered the expedition closer to their intended target. On the east of the island, where the party was now heading, was the Arctic Cordillera. An immense range of mountains, stone gods of the North.

"What is it?" Aedan leaned from the rear seat to Cikuq, who was actively checking his maps.

"Slow down," Cikuq told the driver.

"What is it, lad?"

"We should be getting close. The village lies on this peninsula. We should be on the lookout for any recent signs of activity."

"Alright," Captain Aedan sat back. As they drew near to the water, they passed several monoliths, stone pillars left in the ice to mark the way. The barren land rolled into the North Atlantic.

"Look, sir," One of the crew pointed out of his window. "Smoke, just over the hill," The truck brought its tracks to a halt and Aedan was the first to proceed on foot. Over the snowdrift, he led the men to where the smoke was originating.

"Holy shit," On the far side of the hill, the skeleton of a village lay dead in the snow. Huts left empty, torn open by years of long winters. Not even ghosts lived in a place so thoroughly dead.

The expedition proceeded down the hill, where the village hung onto the shore. Drifts of snow blended the houses with the narrow lanes beneath. Furniture was lit dimly by the rays of light, coming though the iced over windows.

It was like walking into a model, everything was placed and left as if it would have been used, but the people were missing. There were no bodies, no signs that the nomadic tribe packed and went elsewhere. The haunting corpse of a town left the explorers with deep chills.

Aedan went to the house, where the smoke was. This building was cleared off, unlike the rest, and was in the best shape of them all. The captain walked in without a word; instantly greeted by the warmth of a wood-burning stove. He saw a cot with a sleeping bag and a hefty pack on the floor.

"Get some more wood for this fire," He called to his small crew, after stepping outside. "See if there are any more houses we can use for a few nights."

"Is he here?" Cikuq asked privately.

"He will be."

The men broke into a second house and started a fire. While the rest of the crew hunkered in, Aedan stood, keeping watch on the far hill. The wind began to pick up as the night was forming. One of the men brought Aedan a cup of coffee and implored him to get inside soon. His captain didn't listen. Even after temperatures dropped below negative thirty, Aedan was too obsessed with finding this man to give up.

"There you are, you bastard," He finally muttered through his binoculars. In the dark howling snowfall, a silhouette formed. Aedan stayed brooding on the hilltop, waiting.

As the man trudged closer, his image became clearer. His navy parka collected ice on the fur, his legs were wrapped in hide, mukluk boots. He had a spear in hand for the fish he had in a sling across his shoulder. This man had a frosted beard and brown curly hair.

Clairvoyant

Tiguaak

Ezekiel Cacheman opened up a journal and handed it to Captain Aedan. The rest of the crew huddled around the walls of the small shack, trying to stay warm in the polar night.

"Whoever owned this, disappeared with the rest of the tribe," Zeke started to explain his findings. "He wrote about being here, in Kivitoo. It sounded like he lived here for some time, but then his notes just stopped. Check the date, it's around the time that legend says it should be: early nineteen-hundreds."

"Why was this-" Aedan looked for a name that the journal was bound to. "-guy living here in the first place?"

"It sounds like he was hunting walrus for their tusks. What is interesting is in the last few pages, he talks about hearing rumors of a mammoth being spotted during an Inuit hunt. Now I have no idea whether that's connected or not to the disappearance, but he seemed very interested in finding it."

"A mammoth? Like a forty-thousand-year-old mammoth?"

"That's what's written," Zeke defended the improbable, then turned to shuffle through his pack. "And up until recently, I also only thought they were rumors until I found this," He pulled out an object, wrapped in leather, slightly bigger than the size of his hand. Ezekiel removed the wrappings to reveal a white rock-like object with dark, horizontal lines across one of the faces. "It's a mammoth tooth."

"So, what's your next move? Just live out here the rest of your life and hope an elephant doesn't trample you in your sleep?" Aedan scoffed at Zeke and his fossil.

"Maybe, not every exploration needs to be a crusade. I'll keep roaming wherever the wind pushes me. What's another five years in exile?" Zeke said frankly. "I don't know what you want from me, captain. I don't know why you came all this way to find me. Maybe curiosity, I don't know. I'm not looking for a place to settle down. I'm not looking for anything, not seeking fame. I'm just wandering, I guess."

"Some eskimo chief told us you were this grand explorer, to find you're just another homeless bastard," Aedan dropped the journal to the cement. "We'll leave you to it then," He turned to his men in the room as he left. Aedan smirked privately, content that he still felt superior, now receiving affirmation that he was still the "best" in his mind. The crew left Zeke alone in the house. They huddled against one another as they braved the harshness of the outdoors.

Ezekiel now picked up the journal and began to read from his marked page, studying the sketches of the primeval behemoth. He flipped through the tome until he fell asleep that night.

The death of winter was omnipresent in the Arctic Circle. The wind howled like wolves, tearing at houses, looking to blow them down. Fangs of ice were left hanging of roofs after nights of relentless attack.

The wolf haunted him in his dreams. It tried to break his spirit slowly, leaving him as a pile of dry bones. Ezekiel would wake up with the night sweats and feared the killer was still out there. The ancient wolf, brushed in my blood, was resurrected every winter. It hunted the man, and for five years, Zeke could not see one without the other.

Water steamed as Ezekiel brewed his tea in the warm of morning. Sweet honey filled the air with its aroma, providing comfort to the worn man, who looked old for thirty. The sun had not yet made it appearance; however, the moon lit the atmosphere with its pale blue light.

Zeke set out as he did most days, to find food. He became quite proficient in spear hunting the way the natives taught him. Yet foraging was harsh, competing with the other predators. Wolves stalked most of the prey on the land and bears roamed the iced shores. Ezekiel had to become craftier than the natural hunters.

Lakes and bays in the region were frozen solid, but as the moon pulls the tide of the water, so too does it pull the ice. For a few evenings a month, around the full moon, the sea ice would be pulled high enough to crawl under. There, would be a plethora of mussels, waiting on the bottom of the exposed lake. A secret the Inuits also taught him. Zeke nearly expected to find fish frozen in the blocks of ice as well, but never found any.

However, spring was soon approaching. In a month or two the Earth would melt, and rivers of life would flow again. Yet, winter does not like to go quietly. It would leave like a lion, roaring until the bitter end.

Over the covered ground, Zeke pushed onward. He was never afraid of getting lost, "just find the shore and follow it back to the village," was his philosophy. Leading him further, was the hope of finding tracks. With the journal in hand, Ezekiel was also out to find a giant. Not to hunt it, but to simply discover it. Any imprint in the snow was a possible sign of the mammoth.

He lived on local legends: the unknown. There were no new continents to uncover, no maps left to be made, but there is always more out there. The illusion that man had discovered everything, simply by having the globe mapped out, kept explorers grounded on chains. Zeke knew this, I had seen the wonderment in him. There will always be one thing more in God's creation than we would ever uncover. No matter how far or deep, there was always something more out there, hiding, lurking in the deepest abyss of our world. This is what fueled him after five years. The only thing stable about this life of adventure was the constant acknowledgment of the unknown.

The perilous wind picked up snow from the mountains and hurled it across the valley. A roar like a hurricane seemed to echo against the stone. "Further," Ezekiel chanted to himself. The storm flogged the man, beating him relentlessly with heavy ice and razor winds. A shadow came and went in his vision. He pushed through the snow, frantically trying to catch up. The silhouette was veiled beneath the unholy amount of snowfall. It faded in and out of sight, almost taunting Zeke.

"Where are you?" He clenched his teeth. "Why won't you show yourself, huh? You drove me out here and of course, you are nowhere to be seen! 'If I go to the east,'" He began to quote. "'He is not there; if I go to the west, I do not find him. When he is at work in the north, I do not see him; when he turns to the south, I catch no glimpse of him.' No matter where in the compass I go, you're not there. You made me a castaway, didn't you? Ripped me from the fold!" He called into the clouds. His father taught him how to pray when Zeke was a kid, but that language was gone, those ritualistic words didn't communicate what he was feeling. "I don't know what you want anymore."

As he continued to get closer, he heard its cries and saw its shape, as if it had fallen down. Ezekiel ran on top of the snow to reach it.

"It's the mammoth man!" As Zeke approached, he saw that the shadow was the expedition crew, huddled around each other.

"Cikuq? Aedan? What are you doing here?"

"We tried to leave but the truck broke through the ice," The Inuit shouted over the gales. "We couldn't get everyone out. Johannsson, our driver, was stuck. The water, it was just too frigid to dive in after him."

"Is everyone else okay?" Zeke asked them.

"Everyone else was able to get out through the back before the Sno-Cat sank." Cikuq declared. Aedan stepped behind his men.

"You left him there as it was sinking?" Ezekiel turned the captain of the crew.

"We had no choice, lad! He was stuck. Better him than both of us," Aedan challenged.

"You coward!" Zeke was met with a punch to the jaw.

"You have no stock in this, bastard!" Aedan spat between his teeth. "This is *my* crew, you didn't have to make the choice, I did. But now it seems we're lost, and you are going to get us out of here!"

Zeke couldn't find the words to respond. Arguing wasn't going to help his position. Therefore, he pointed onward and led the parade back toward the coastline, through the mountain pass. The snow began to fall even more heavily and soon all vision was lost.

"I can't see," The men began to yell. "Where are you?"

"Owen put that camera away and help us!"

"Here! Everyone, come here!" Zeke turned back and shouted into the whiteout. He staggered through the deep powder. "Come here!" The men all eventually stumbled to Zeke. "Grab the belt of the person in front of you. We're going to take this slow."

"Slow? We need to get out of here now!" Aedan opposed.

"By all means, go your own way. Everyone else, on me!" Zeke began to lead the crew once again. Each man holding onto the one in front of them. Infuriated that his crew listened to orders from someone else, Aedan split and ran ahead.

They plowed through the snow; breaking through the ever-increasing barrier. Eventually, Aedan's tracks disappeared, which Ezekiel was initially following. Onward and onward, they pushed into the storm, restlessly beating on them.

"How does he know where to go?" One of the men called. "He has no compass." Zeke heard this but paid it no mind. He was confident that he was heading east, toward the sea. Even as ice built up around his eyes, and snow covered his vision, Ezekiel was led by instinct.

One of the men fell from exhaustion. His hands we so stricken with frost that his grip remained firm on his comrade. The frost had been eating at everyone's flesh, making it difficult to let go. Soon, all the men had fallen, being pulled down from the one behind them. They lost their feet and were crawling to orient themselves.

"Come on! Get up, all of you!" Zeke howled. "We need to keep moving!" The small team pulled themselves back up.

"Sir, look!" One man cried. Face down, half buried, was Captain Aedan. The crew rushed over to him, flipping him over.

"He's still breathing," Zeke muttered as he put his ear to Aedan's mouth. "Help me, get him up!" Several men hoisted him into their arms and carried him through the blizzard.

For miles, they went over the frozen Earth, until they reached the sea ice. As Zeke had planned, they went south to find the village. They brought Aedan into the house and set him by the wood-burning stove, since he was still unconscious.

"What's the plan now?" Cikuq asked openly. The house was silent.

"We may have to walk back," One of the older men in the group spoke up.

"Aye, we may have to. We've no vehicle or equipment."

"We could see if there's a boat in the village. Pick it out of the ice and row back."

"The boat would be rotten by now. Besides, the ice would be much for us."

"No way am I getting into some tiny rig, I'll stay right here on land," The men began to bicker among themselves.

"Mr. Cikuq is the local here, let him decide."

"Okay," He sighed. Cikuq pulled out his map of Baffin Island, where they were. "We're in Kivitoo, right here. There's another village on the water, maybe thirty, forty miles south. That's if we cut across the sea ice."

"That's a couple days walk, not that bad." One of the men added.

"Across the ice, will that be safe?"

"The sea is as solid as stone. We may be burly men, but I'm sure we wouldn't break through!" The larger man in the party roared out in laughter.

"No, but there are bears." Cikuq added. "Polar bears hunt on the ice. We'd be walking exposed, in their territory for two or three days. Yet, I don't see a better way."

"What do you think, Cacheman? You've been surviving out here for a few years. What do you think is best?" Zeke leaned forward from where he was against the wall.

"I agree with Cikuq. You would need to walk across the ice."

After the men all nestled in for the night, Cikuq went and sat down next to Zeke on his cot.

"Why don't you come with us?" Before he could answer Cikuq continued. "It isn't right for someone to live completely alone their whole life. Plus, if I am assuming correctly about you, you like to live for some adventure."

"And your captain won't mind?"

"It's an empty title, but he likes to give orders and feel in charge. If you wanted to come, he couldn't stop you. Plus, I think our crew needs some good, hardy men who've been around the world. You think about it."

A few days later, after the storm abated, the men prepared for their crucible march. Ezekiel rolled up his blankets and packed his bag. Then he stepped out the door with the rest, leaving only an old axe behind.

Out on the open ice, the wind would be more unbearable. The men were completely at the mercy of Mother Nature's unbiased killing pattern. The men pulled their gear on a dogsled, graciously provided by the remains of the village. After so many miles of walking, the legs become numb, almost forgetting they're moving at all. The vapor from each breath clouds the vision, more so than the shining snow already did.

"We should break for camp," The older man suggested. Blue-grey skies dimmed as the sun fell behind the mountains to the west. "I dare not carry on in the dark."

"Aye," The others agreed as they dropped the reigns and collapsed into the snow.

"What do we do now?" Aedan asked.

"Dig," Zeke said as he was already getting the shovel from the sled. "Unless you would rather sleep in the open air. Just, uh, don't dig too deep," He chuckled.

The others dug their trenches into the snow. Owen O'Donnell, the cameraman, panned the scene, capturing the vastness of the world around them. They were truly in no man's land.

Zeke drilled down and then into the snow beside him. Building quinzhees was a skill he had picked up when we were scouts together, but after years of living in the arctic circle, it had become his trade. He directed the other men with their shelters; all who were wise, listened. Aedan, characteristically, believed in his own way of doing things.

As the sun vanished, the northern skies appeared. The magnificent stars had been stolen away and polluted by big cities. But out there, in the very crest of human civilization, the lights were unadulterated. A streak of red flashed itself. Then green and blue followed. The ancient powers illuminated the Earth. Red, green, blue, all telling a story; a tale of fiery destruction and restoration. As if the ribbons were God's own glorious aura.

"Woah," Ezekiel saw these whirling lights and was tempted to wake the other men but decided to cherish them alone.

It seemed a miracle that all the men lasted the night. The construction of their shelters held in their body heat. When the dawn greeted the Earth again, the men were already on the move. The morning stars, however, were not the only lights. Over east, from the sea, flashing lights caught the men's eyes.

"A ship!"

"Get the flares," Aedan ordered. They scrambled to the sled and found their stash. Aedan lit one and began to wave it around, jumping like a madman. Several others followed his example and ignited their scarlet lights. The boat, now in clearer view, flashed its searchlight at the party.

"We're bloody saved!"

The Zenith

The explorers were brought to the vessel from the ice by a small dinghy. Even inside the ship, the sub-zero temperatures seemed to creep in through the metal, asbestos-lined hull. In the mess hall, the fishermen meet timidly with Aedan and his men. The chef brewed coffee for everyone, huddled around the now overcrowded room. The six explorers near doubled the fishing crew.

"Nice boat," Aedan attempted to start small talk with the sailors.

"Aye, that she is. The Zenith is a, um, mighty fine ship," The chef answered, trying to make the environment more comfortable. "Uh, kaffi?" He put out the fresh pot of coffee. Each party preferred to talk quietly with their own crew than converse with the others.

"So, you guys were on a hike?" One fisherman took a jab.

"Close," Zeke answered with a chuckle.

"We're explorers," Aedan began is practiced introduction. "With the Royal Geographical Society. Traversing and filming the great arctic!"

"Filming?" The ship's crew seemed to liven up, exchanging glances and readjusting their seats.

"Oh, yes," Owen, the Irishman, responded. "Filming a document'ry." The sailors glanced at each other more frequently and with uneasy expressions.

"What are you men fishing for?" Cikuq inquired after a few minutes of awkward silence.

"Halibut," An old sailor nearly interrupted his crewmate.

"Catch a lot this time of year, then?"

"Fair amount, not too much ice in the way," The old man was stern in his voice.

"That's true," Cikuq concluded. The sea ice had been starting to melt already, with spring soon around the corner.

Afterwards, the sailors departed back to their posts, leaving the explorers to themselves in the mess hall, where they would have to sleep until they got back to port.

"Ezekiel," Cikuq waved him over to the corner, where he was standing.

"Yeah?" Zeke asked as he was looking around.

"I don't think this is a fishing boat," Cikuq said quietly.

"What do you mean?"

"Commercial fishing shouldn't start until April. Plus, these men seem on edge with us around, especially when we said we were filming."

"I did notice that," Zeke agreed. "What do you think is going on then?"

"I'm not sure."

From across the room, Aedan observed Zeke.

"I'm weary of that man," he said under his breath.

"What of?" His crewmate asked, not taking his gaze off of the cup of coffee he was sipping. "Seems to have done nothing wrong. He's got a real spirit of adventure."

"He's been surviving away from civilization for five years. A man like that's on the run. Must've done something pretty bad if he's been running for so long."

"I don't even feel bad for him," Jack said to Allan during my funeral. "He did this, you know?"

"Yeah," From behind the service, a loud engine fired up. A handful turned to see that Rick took off in his pickup, presumably after he finished smoking his cigarette. Eventually, everyone left after saying their goodbyes. Joe and his parents were the last ones to leave before Zeke, but even he didn't say anything to his old friend.

It wasn't before long the cherry red Jeep was sitting out on the yard. 'FOR SALE: HAS ISSUES.' I assume my parents were selling it to pay for the arrangements, as well as to cleanse their life from this new baggage they've been handed.

Weeks went by and no one checked to see if Zeke was okay. No one checked to see if anyone else was okay. Everyone sunk into their own lives, devoting themselves to their work. The story of a young man dying in the Boundary Waters Canoe Area made local news and eventually Zeke couldn't go anywhere in Duluth without getting glares or thrown out.

"No one wants you here," Jack spoke plainly when Ezekiel came to his door. "You killed Lane. Maybe not on purpose, but you drove him out into the wild with you. This was your fault and now you have to pay for it. There are consequences in the real world. Not ones you can run away from, because they always come back," Zeke didn't answer. "We went looking for you, you know? Us guys spent some days running after you, searching the trail. Had others driving around in their cars."

"Yeah?"

"Oh, yeah. We probably spent a week out on the trail, slowing giving up on you. We cared about you a lot and it's really shitty that you didn't. You were my best friend and then you left without telling anyone. You should've told us, brought us into it," Jack wiped his eyes with his sleeve. "It would have been better if you died instead of him. That way other people aren't paying for your arrogance. You're no better than Boone," Jack cut at him. "You should have never come back."

"You have family?" Cikuq asked Zeke, getting him back from wherever his mind drifted to.

"Not anymore, no." He shook his head. "You?"

"Not of my own. I have a lot of relatives back in Quebec. I guess I felt forced into a life of isolation."

"I get that."

"I'm sure you do," Cikuq chuckled as he tried to slurp his coffee with the motion of the ship. "You and I are both called adventurers, pulled into this life for whatever reason. Both of us galvanized by something, it may be something different, but nonetheless, there's something that's driving us into this lifestyle. To settle down would inhibit a man from roaming freely."

"That's one way to put it," Zeke smirked. His attention was turned when he heard the men outside begin to shout. Through the porthole, Zeke saw sailors ran across the deck. The ship began to turn quickly, silverware slid off the table as the boat rolled. Zeke stood to get a better look outside. "Harpoons."

"What?" Cikuq shot up. Sailors threw themselves against the taffrail and began to shoot into the water with their weapons. Gunsmoke tainted the mist from the sea, making the air foul.

"They're not hunting halibut," Zeke moved over to let Cikuq see the orca that the men were shooting at. The black fish was screeching with each bullet in its spine. Blood stained its beautiful black and white markings. "Is that legal here? I was a part of a tribal hunt once, but is something like this allowed?"

"Not in Canadian waters, only the Inuits have that right." Looking up, Zeke noticed Owen with his camera against another porthole, filming the whale hunt. "Owen," He scolded. "If those men know that you recorded them, who knows what they will do to us."

"Aye, sir." The burly man replied, taking down his tripod. Glancing back out the window, Zeke saw the fishermen raise their net. In it, a bloodied killer whale suspended in the lines. Countless bullet holes drained its blood onto the non-skid deck.

"Cikuq," Zeke warned as he saw the young man conspire with rage, gripping the door.

"We need to do something. This cannot go on," The sailors outside unloaded their net and dumped the steaming carcass into a hatch below deck.

"Then we wait, there's nothing we can do now. They still drive the ship. We can turn in the ships information when we get back to land. If we fight back now, they'll throw us overboard. Who knows?"

"Yes, but I will not allow another one to die."

The next morning's air was brisk and refreshing. The rush of waves against the hull was enough to dampen the rumble of the engine. Through the arctic waters, The Zenith passed between titans of ice.

The giants lay patiently in calm oceans, easily dwarfing the ship. Larger than anything man could every construct, the icebergs ruled the northern seas. With the melting of glaciers in the spring, more icebergs were plunged into the ocean. The relatively tiny vessel had no choice but to carry on through the maze.

Ezekiel stood at the bow, enjoying the stillness of the world. Each breath, he took in the salty aroma of the ocean. Not even the vapor from his mouth could ruin the scene surrounding him. He fixed his gaze on the multitude of icebergs, strikingly white against the pure, sapphire water.

"Fetching, no?" A sailor came to approach him.

"Yeah, it really is." Even though the men were still layered in their coats, the cold wasn't bitter. "It's quite relaxing out here."

"Aye," The old sailor leaned on the railing next to Ezekiel. "I grew up on these waters, here. Papa would have me as his deckhand, fish right off Baffin Bay. Name's Erling, so you know."

"Ezekiel. Suppose you've seen a lot of whales then?" Zeke questioned intently. "Love to see one for myself."

"Aye…" He kept his eyes on the water. "Lots of killers and minkes. Lovely creatures."

"Oi!" Another sailor called from the top deck. "We spotted an-" He noticed Zeke and began to stammer. "An, uh, a storm closing in. Best you head on inside," Zeke shot a glare at the men and went back into the vessel.

"We shouldn't have picked them up, they'll for sure get us put away," Erling bickered as they ran back to the stern.

"Nevermind them, this fish is a monster. Nearly as long as the boat!"

"The boat?" He paused before running to the weather deck.

"Hit her with the harpoon!" A tall man with black dreadlocks ordered, as the crew was firing rounds at the whale.

"Its blubber's too thick, we can't spear it!" Men shouted over the splashing of water. The black whale would rise to get a breath and descend back into the depths, but the ship stayed right on top of it.

"Shoot the dammed thing," The tall man, took a rifle and began unloading into the whale. Its tail threw waves, leaving powerful wakes that rocked the ship. Pneumatic spears fired from the taffrail couldn't seem to pierce the creatures hide. "Keep us on her!" He yelled into radio, intended for the helmsman. The ship veered dangerously close to ice as they tried to follow the sea creature. Even if it dived beneath the monstrous icebergs, it would need to rise for air at some point.

"Can't get a good shot, Gudmundur!" As the sailor was going in to aim the harpoon another time, he was shoved aside.

"What are you doing?" Cikuq yelled and ran toward the commotion. "You can't hu-" The Captain hit him with the stock of his gun.

220

"Hey!" Ezekiel hollered, charging out onto the deck. Aedan stepped back, staying out of the situation.

"Don't, son," He was stopped by the fisherman he spoke to earlier. Zeke pushed back as he saw Captain Gudmundur kick Cikuq down again, then fire another shot at the whale.

"What the hell?" Ezekiel stormed forward.

"Leave it be!" Gudmundur turned and aimed his gun at Zeke. He took one step toward the tall man and was knocked out. Cikuq stumbled inside.

The whale kept running. "Well, get on with you!" The Captain yelled at the men, who stood in awe of his actions. "Huh?" He screamed. "Get on with it!" Erling put his rile on his shoulder and carried Ezekiel inside. The captain emptied his gun into the back of the leviathan, but it escaped into the deep.

"We told you, Captain, we should have never taken them on," The whaling crew stood around the tall man in the bridge, where he steered the ship.

"Now we've beaten two of their men," Another sighed.

"Do not challenge my orders!" Gudmundur snapped. "We rescued them and now they need to face the reality they're in. We don't make money being soft. Tomorrow, we'll 'rive at port and we'll let them go. And *none* of this will interfere with selling our goods. They don't know where we caught the whales, they never ask. The townsfolk at Nuuk know our trade."

"Sir, this just isn't what we signed up for," Erling sighed.

"No?" The Captain accused. "I suppose you thought this was a cruise line. Yer whalers for Chrissake, now man up and do your damn job!"

"Aye, aye," He said between his teeth.

"How's your head?" Erling, the old sailor asked Zeke as he walked into the med bay. His broad figure filled the doorframe of the stuffy little room.

"Hurts," He said plainly, holding an ice pack to it. Cikuq was beside him, also tending to his wounds.

"I, uh, I'm sorry for what happened. Captain Gudmundur can be a bit extreme," Neither one said anything. "Look, we'll be in port tomorrow. I'll help you contact the authorities and then you can be off."

"Helping us report you?" Zeke acknowledged. The old man stepped into the room and closed the hatch.

"I never wanted any of this, never wanted to be whaling illegally for a living. I'm just a fisher by trade. Now that doesn't excuse what I've done, but I can at least do this right. Let me do this for you."

Greenland?" Aedan demanded. "What happened to going to Quebec?" None of the sailors around him on the docks answered to him. They were disinterested and too occupied unloading The Zenith of its corpses. "Hey, you were supposed to take us back to Quebec! Where's your captain?"

"Sir," Aedan's crew called for him. "We're heading into town to find us an inn to stay at," The men walked up from the harbor in the warm afternoon sunlight.

Nuuk was a comely city built on the sea. Its buildings stuck out from the rocky hillscape like watchmen. Each house was painted with bright colors of reds, greens, and blues. Yellow churches were dotted in the mix. The quiet streets and warm shops welcomed the worn explorers into this dreamy little town. Owen quickly made his way to the top of the hill to film the colorful seaside, panning the world.

"There," Erling hung up the pay phone. "Reported the ship. Now, if you gentlemen don't mind, I better be getting a move on back home."

"Not going back to your crew?" Cikuq asked the old man.

"After committing mutiny? No, sir," He sighed. "I'm sorry again, lads, for everything. If ever you need something, I have a cottage just over in Kapisillit, on the ocean. That's where I'll be."

"We appreciate it," Zeke spoke for the both of them. "Thank you."

After exchanging their money at the bank and avoiding questions about how they got into the country, the explorers found a dingy pub to unwind in. The refreshing air outside was contrasted heavily by the dark atmosphere inside the bar.

"If you must know, lassie," One of the men began to tell the waitress, who was supplying the explorers with plenty of ale. "We were exploring arctic Canada for a number of months. You know, fighting bears and uh..."

"Bollocks!" Another cried. "You never fought a bear."

"You've come to explore the unsettled wilderness of Nuuk, then?" The waitress picked.

"Captain Aedan come quick! We found the perfect girl for ya!" The men laughed.

"Well, eventually we found, this guy," He put his arm around Ezekiel, who was quite a bit tamer than the rest. "He's been surviving out in the arctic for- how long did you say you've been livin' up there?"

"Well, about two years total in Canada. But, five years on the road altogether. Gone all across America, survived out in the Rocky Mountains for a while," The young waitress glanced at Zeke as she went to hand off another beer.

"Yeah, he may have us in years, but in scars, I may have you all!" Another joined in, competing for the young lady's attention. This man hoisted his leg onto the bar counter and revealed a long, narrow mark in his flesh.

"Fishing hook?" Zeke mocked. The others laughed as the older man refuted, taking his foot down.

"Well what about you, boy? You got any better?"

At first, he shook his head, then Zeke pulled up his left sleeve. "I may have tangled with a bear or two, but wolves left me with the biggest scars," The outline of teeth took up most of Ezekiel's forearm. Time had healed the broken bone but left the rugged tissue. The other men sat for a moment in awe.

"Aye, but what of tattoos?" The men roared as they continued to overshadow each other. Zeke moved over to Cikuq and Owen, who were enjoying the charade from afar.

"I think you have an admirer," Owen pointed at the waitress, who was caught looking at Ezekiel again.

"What of it?" He chuckled.

"Look at this place, this town's gorgeous. What better place to settle down? Ezekiel, you've been trying to survive five years. How is that living? I can't imagine how exhausting that is fer ya. You don't have to keep going, you can be done."

"I think I've given up the idea of settling down a long while ago. I'm restless. Plus, I've never been good with a lady," He sipped from his pint.

"Well, say you scored a date with the lass."

"Say I what?" Zeke nearly spit out his drink as Owen got up and went to the waitress.

"I will add, although me and my people are much against alcohol, it is *very* entertaining to watch," Cikuq laughed as he looked at his water, then put it back his bruised forehead. "What if he has a point?"

"What do you mean?" Zeke looked over.

"You know yourself better than I do, but this little hamlet seems like the perfect place to rest and settle down for a while. Who knows, maybe you'll find a lady who likes to travel, better yet who even likes you!" The men chuckled. Zeke looked up at the young waitress, who had her frizzy black hair tied up. "Look, all we're saying is that you can't close the door on the idea. You don't *need* to be running your whole life."

"I don't know. I don't think it's for me. Settling down, starting a family may be something I have to give up. Like you said, it inhibits us," Cikuq rolled his eyes at his own words coming back to him.

"We're just worried for you. I never really thought of how hard all those years must have been. You may think that it's something that you're required to give up, but it's not. You're right here, you can stop running. No one is chasing you, telling you that you have to do this. You *can* be done. If getting away from your home was what you wanted, here you are. We're probably going to be here a few days, just think about it."

"Okay," He sighed. "Okay," Since leaving, Zeke had not made a single relationship for means other than survival. Making Cikuq and Owen acquaintances was pushing new territory for the man.

At the end of the night, when the men were taking their tabs, Zeke found a girl's name on his receipt, followed by three pairs of numbers. He decided to take a walk down to the pier while the others were stumbling across the street to the inn. Aedan could be heard asking them where they've been. The ocean was dimly lit by the lighthouses, where Ezekiel found himself resting.

Staring into the sea was good for thinking. The grey water roared against the rocks and the cement. Beacons brought forth by the lighthouses seemed to protect the vulnerable young man like watchmen.

"What are you gonna do?" Joe asked, as Zeke looked into Lake Superior from the pier down on Park Point.

"Leave," He didn't take his eyes off of the November whitecaps, the gales blew back is hair. "I can't stay here anymore. No one wants me here, Joe."

"Where would you go?"

"Anywhere, I just can't be in Duluth anymore. I can't help but to feel that I need to be elsewhere."

"Someone would think that after what happened, you would be done with adventures," Joe said solemnly.

"I wouldn't consider this an adventure. This is running away. God's thrown me into exile. You're right though. I don't think people would expect me to want to travel any more, but they sure don't want me around."

"Give them time."

"I will, and space. I'll give them what they need to move on," He paused. "I'll be gone in the morning and soon enough, everyone in Duluth will forget about me," The young man pushed off from the concrete he was leaning against.

"What about us? I know Jack and the rest of them are mad at you, but we're your friends. They'll forgive you eventually. How will you be able to have any friends or anyone in your life if you always run?"

"Didn't think you would call," Joann, the waitress from the other night, said as she met up with Zeke on the boardwalk. The afternoon light was warming up the town.

"I suppose I needed some stubborn old men to persuade me," He chuckled. "So, how long have you lived in Nuuk?"

"Whole life, not a lot of places here to escape to. And what about you, you're from the States, right?" She adjusted her hair, which she wore down that day.

"Yeah, lived there mostly, but, um, moved around a lot."

"Why's that?"

"Just can't sit still for very long, needed to be traveling. I like seeing new places," Zeke responded vaguely after some hesitation.

"I would love that, be out in the world, seeing all the big cities, like Rome or New York. Or taking a cruise around the oceans!" Joann lost herself in daydreams. "I'm sure you've been everywhere. I bet you know at least one person in every city!"

"Not exactly," Ezekiel scratched his head. "I, uh, do a lot more camping. To get away from big cities."

"Oh, well, I'm sure you've seen plenty that way too," She looked down and lightly kicked a pebble off the boardwalk.

"I suppose I have, yeah," He paused. "So, Jo, what's there to see in Greenland?"

"Nothing, no cities, no people," She paused. "I'm sure it's your kind of place," She smiled and nudged playfully.

"Sounds like it. Any cool hikes or just places to see the glaciers?"

"I'm sure there are, never really been though."

"How could you not? It's practically in your backyard?" Zeke exclaimed.

"Just haven't, but if you ever need a tour guide, I could get familiar with the trails really quick," She winked. They continued around the seaside, stopping at shops, and overlooking the ocean. "You religious?" She inquired for the sake of conversation.

"Used to be. Father's a priest," Ezekiel shared. "I think God and I leave each other alone, right now."

"Huh. So, where will you all be off to next?" She left the topic.

"I think the crew will probably go back to Quebec. We've, uh, gotten pretty off course coming here."

"It sure sounds like that. Will you go with them?"

"I don't know," Zeke looked out into the water. "I certainly could, but-"

"Prefer to be on your own?" She asked before Ezekiel could finish his sentence.

"It's just what I'm used to. Never liked big crowds. They're fine, they just travel a bit differently than I'd like, besides I don't think their captain cares for me all that much."

"So, in theory," She dragged her words on. "You *could* stay in Nuuk."

"In theory," Zeke smirked, which didn't give her the satisfying answer she wanted. "I think I may still travel around, keep living off the grid. There are a lot of cities for me to avoid over in Europe."

"All on your own, though?"

"No, I think I have a few in mind who may want to come with," Joann was hopeful, but Zeke was really thinking of the men he'd come to know.

"Well, do you think you would ever wind up back here?"

"Guess I'll see, never been one to retrace my steps," To which she didn't know how to react any longer. "You're lovely, Jo, but I'm a restless, rambling man. I would love to stay here, in this beautiful city, but I can't. It would hurt me more than anything to stay in one place, at least for now."

"What are you trying to escape?" Joann said, disheartened.

"You know, at this point," Zeke began. "I don't know. I think the best thing for me, I realized, is to travel, experience novelty. I'm uncomfortable with the familiar, mundane routine. I was always scared of being tied down by what society wanted of me. What I need to be comfortable is some unknown."

"So, you left her?" Owen said, speaking up to Zeke, who was walking up the green hillside.

"Well, I took her back home, if that's what you're asking, but I told her I wasn't going to stay."

"And you think that's best?" Cikuq asked from behind. Zeke stopped on the trail and turned back toward the two.

"Do you think it's for the best that you both left the expedition and your jobs to come with me?"

"Well, uh, of course lad!" Owen began to stammer. "We never liked that wicked man. Although the whaling captain may give Aedan a run for his money!"

Erling sat on the front porch of his bungalow, overlooking the salty bay, which was white with chunks of melting ice. The old man was enjoying the cool morning coffee, in a black wool pullover. Spring air was fresh and full of dew. White flowers started to show themselves after a long winter of hiding.

"Top of the morning!" Owen called. The old man set down his mug and turned his head to us.

"Well that didn't take long, you find yourselves in trouble again?"

"We may, yet," Zeke smirked. "How are you Erling?"

"Mighty fine," He coughed through his husky white beard. "So, what are you conniving this morning?"

"We split with the rest of the crew. They all headed back to Canada, calling off the rest of the expedition, but we're gonna keep roaming along. Plus, we have all the film equipment," Owen said and turned, showing the wooden tripod strapped to his pack.

"Figured we would offer to take you along, since you've been recently unemployed," Ezekiel stated. Erling chewed on his jaw, thinking.

"You just want my boat, don't you?" The old man eventually laughed.

"No, come on," The men began to protest. "We would never invite you if it were just for the boat. But hey, now that you mention it, that would be really useful."

"Save it, boys," Erling grunted, as he struggled to get up from his wooden chair. "Let me get my things."

"Just like that?" Cikuq asked, looking at his companions, who were equally surprised.

"Don't know if you noticed," He called from his empty, one-room cottage. "I don't exactly have a lot going on here."

Going down the cobble stairs to the water, the men went onto the dock and into the sizeable sailboat. The chipped white paint of the vessel reflected the man who drove her; old and withered, but strong at the core. The cabin below deck was dusty, yet free from clutter. It seemed Erling never cared to own many items. "So, this film you're making?" He asked Owen, who was being particularly cautious with his bag.

"Basically, we're making a documentary about what life is like in the arctic. That's why we started o'er in Canada, filming the Inuit people there. Guess it ain't all bad that we ended up here by accident, been getting plenty of footage. Which is why we're pining to keep going with the expedition; wanted to see more."

"There's truly nothing better than seeing the world. I can definitely show you around Greenland and Iceland, take you to the coastal towns. There'll be a thing or two worth seeing, I'm sure."

"Wherever you want to take us, that'll be alright. I'm not one for setting the course," Zeke found a rack to lay down on.

"Alright, well give me a bit, then we'll be ready to launch," Erling went back up on deck.

That afternoon, the ship pushed off from the dock. The white vessel passed between the fjords, towering cliffs on each side of the channel. Erling weaved the ship between the islands in the delta. They eventually came to pass Nuuk. The colorful town grew smaller behind them like a patch of spring flowers against the hills. Canvas sails were hoisted up and caught the wind of the Labrador Sea.

Owen stood on the bow, trying to keep his camera steady as they rolled over the ocean waves, filming the miraculous countryside. Cikuq and Erling were in the bridge, discussing their lives and debating who's endured colder winters. Cikuq was younger but based his arguments on having to endure the hardships of Inuit life in the tundra. Erling, by far, had seen more winters and lived further north. Whether the men meant to escalate their stories of frozen winters or not, didn't seem to impact the exponential course of their conversation.

Ezekiel was also in the bridge, getting lost in the maps; tracing his fingers along the topography, like braille. Mountains rose from the parchment, valleys dipped into the table, and water rolled off onto the floorboard. He tended to always believe there was greener grass no matter where he was. Somewhere in the world was something more beautiful than anything he'd seen yet. Not that he didn't appreciate the beauty of the world he saw, but there was an emptiness in his chest, a longing to see the full potential of God's creation. He longed to satisfy this hunger.

"You'll get lost reading all those maps," An older man said to Zeke from across the counter.

"Pretty sure I can figure out where I'm going," Zeke said as he continued studying the atlas in the breakfast diner.

"Where's that, then?"

"West," The man shook his head and went back to reading his newspaper. "Have a good day," said the young man in the red and black flannel. Zeke grabbed his pack and headed out to a rusty red Cherokee to continue driving into the Rocky Mountains.

Clairvoyant

The Land of Fire and Ice

Waves flooded over the taffrail; water poured in faster than it could flow off. With each crashing wave, the sailboat was drenched, and Zeke with it. The boat rolled and pitched over the stormy ocean. A whitecap came and knocked Ezekiel onto the deck. He slid back toward the bridge until the line around his waist lost slack and yanked him backward.

"You alright there?" Erling called from the helm, though his voice could barely be heard over the rain. Zeke struggled to pull himself back to his feet, seeing the scratches on his arms and face. A wave concussed from behind, throwing the man back down. Ezekiel eventually made it back to the bow and wrapped his arms around the railing.

"Ice!" He called back. "Port side!" From the left, the tide brought in a sizeable amount of ice, that slammed into the hull.

"Dammit!" Erling spat. The ship dipped with the rise and fall of the water, soaking Zeke who was tied to the bow, leaving him coated in salt. The men inside the cabin couldn't tell which way was up anymore. They laid in their racks, desperately clinging onto their belongings, trying not to roll off. Zeke was thrown by another wave, twisting his arm that was still wedged in the railing.

"Christ!" He grunted.

"Come on, son," Erling said to himself, as he steered to keep the ship afloat, driving head on with the waves. He muscled the helm, fighting the winds and forces of the ocean.

"More ice!" Ezekiel pointed of to his right. A boulder-sized piece broke on the railing and shattered across the deck. The ginormous waves bombarded the ship without end. Ezekiel gasped in between hits, wiping his face and brushing back his hair. The storm was miles wide with no end in sight. Clouds shrouded the entire ocean, covering it all in darkness as if there were no sun. It would be difficult to recall what the earth looked like before. They didn't know the time of day, nor which direction they were predominantly heading. All they knew was the waters that were trying to drag the ship into the sea. They were at the mercy of the storm, more violent than any ocean monster. Water slashed at the vessel, flogging the hull with ice.

Like a thundercrack, the main mast broke and twisted its way off of the ship. The sea stole the sail and took it down to the abyss.

"Water's coming in through the walls!" Cikuq ran up to the bridge. The captain didn't respond, in fear that this was the end of his beloved sailboat. "Erling," He cried again, gripping the railing to keep balance.

"Get your things together. You and Owen meet back up here, we'll take the emergency raft," Erling didn't take his eyes off the sea, his enemy. The ship took another dive through a rogue wave. The undertow pulled out the bow of the ship, now parallel with the waves. The helm couldn't turn fast enough and soon the ship was rolled sideways.

"Blasted!" Owen called as he came from the berthing. All of his gear was on his back.

"Get that raft out!" The old captain pointed.

"What about Ezekiel?"

"I'll worry about him, now go!" From Erling's peripheral, a white locomotive crashed down broke the hull. Shards of ice shot out. As the captain looked, he saw Zeke was knocked unconscious. He hesitated to leave the helm, and with it let go of his precious ship.

"What are you doing?" Cikuq yelled across the deck at Erling, who was working his way up to the bow.

"Get on that raft and go! I'm getting the boy!" He made it up to the front, where he caught Zeke's seemingly lifeless body. The knot that bond him to the railing was soaked and pulled tight. Erling tried to untie the mess and pry it off, but it was too strained. His hands were quickly turning blue in the arctic climate. The ship rolled further and exposed a large cavern in the hull, which was quickly filling. Erling ran back to the bridge, seeing that Owen and Cikuq were already on the raft, floating away.

Erling scrambled through the standing water in the bridge as the ship was steadily sinking. Finally, he found his target and pulled out a knife. He stepped outside and clung to the taffrail as the ship plunged into the ocean. Erling pulled himself down with the ship toward the bow. Zeke was floating above the boat, being towed by the line into the deep. The old man was losing his sight in the freezing black water. His hands followed the railing until he hit the manila line. The rough line was frayed thin. Erling, with a dagger in his hand, slit through the weave and began to pull Ezekiel toward himself as he swam upward.

Erling carried Zeke through the brittle water. Swimming sidestroke with one arm and trying to keep Ezekiel above the waves with the other. The old man, himself, was barely staying afloat. A bolt of light pierced the sky. It whipped back through again and again. The old man grunted as he started swimming faster toward the beam of light.

The lone lighthouse broke the darkness that covered the earth. Erling must have possessed some serious old-man strength in order to have carried Zeke through the ocean and up the basalt cliffside.

"Come on, son," He began compressions as soon as he was in the building. There was a pulse, but no breath in him. "Come on," The old man continued, then blew into the young man's mouth.

"Need me to call anyone?" The keeper brought down dry clothes for the men. Erling didn't answer, he kept pressing on Ezekiel's chest. He took ownership for this because he had asked the young man to be the forward lookout during the storm. "Sir?" Just then, breath came into Zeke's body. He turned over on his side and coughed out water.

"God bless," Ezekiel realized Erling had just pulled him from the grave.

The two men changed into the dry clothes and sat around the wood-burning stove, still trying to warm themselves. In the kitchen, the lighthouse keeper was making them food as well.

"Any idea where we are?"

"Iceland, I assume," Erling replied. "We came in from the North."

"You suppose the others found it to shore?" Ezekiel looked up from his mug, which was used to warm his hands more than anything.

"I don't know, son. I saw them take off with the raft, but I have no idea if they found the shore like we did. My guess is that they would've seen the lighthouse and came here, but they may have drifted a ways too."

"Well, if they don't meet us here, the only other place that I can think of is London."

"London?" Erling coughed.

"Owen and Cikuq are working with the Royal Geographical Society. Their headquarters are in London, so my gut instinct is that they would try to head there."

"Makes sense, I suppose."

"Got a call from the Coast Guard," The keeper interrupted as he came in with stew. "They found your boat; says they want to talk to you. Said they'd be here later tonight."

"Alright, should be no issue," The old man smiled. "Thank you."

As soon as the keeper went back up the tower, Erling got up and made his way to the door.

"Where are you going?" Ezekiel followed him.

"Well, we have one man wanted for whaling and another man who's been traveling around the world without a passport for five years. Seems like a good of a time as any to run," He stole a coat off the rack and went outside into the mist. Having no items left from the ship, Zeke had no issue walking right out of the door.

The two men traversed across the plains, heading south. Springtime air was fresh and new life was forming where snow had previously covered the entire island. The shamrock green pastures rolled on forever, with sturdy mountains rising into the scene. White rivers cut through the fields, carrying brisk glacier water. The streams and waterfalls contrasted the black boulders that peppered the land. The hills never seemed to end, making boundless caves and crags to explore. Wild grass grew thick on the ground and the birds were also populating the skies.

Ezekiel was in his element again. Long hikes, sojourning through foreign fields was where he was most at home. Open blue skies and a sigh of relief on the wind seemed to be all Zeke needed to fuel himself. Like he was a little boy again, hiking with the scouts for the first time. Experiencing the first freedom of flight like an arrow. Ezekiel had just been let out of Eden, now wandering the world for the first time. Man was born in the wilderness; he would be damned if he let himself die back in the garden.

In the night, the men could see a humble barn, lit up by lanterns. These tiny farms were hidden among the great plains. Here, there were only a handful of animals and several garden beds of vegetables. Inside the barn were ponies, thick-coat Icelandic horses, who didn't seem to mind the extra company when Ezekiel and Erling slipped in. Haybales would have to serve as beds for the night.

"Morning," Erling called the next sunrise as they stepped out of the barn and met the man sitting on his porch. The farmer only stared confused and waved as the men were off again. Wind carried cool air off the glaciers, down into the valley where they were. Walking over hills and through brooks, pulling the frontier closer.

In some weird way, life was back in their own hands. As if running was the freedom they needed. Erling spent years trapped on the whaling boat, blackmailed into staying aboard. The old man had not truly been out in the world, where his sailor's heart called him. Ezekiel surely felt that way too, traveling only by means of escape, trying to survive.

Neither one worried, despite being separated from the other two, despite being lost in the world. They hiked pridefully through the beautiful countryside. Like old lions, the men paraded onward. Roaring in the valley, as if it were theirs. Rather, if it were no ones, and they respected just how wild this land was.

In one of the many hillsides, a small A-frame cottage hid from view. Its roof, reaching the ground, was covered in grass. The men would have hiked passed it if it weren't for the dark wooden door that caught their attention.

"Anyone home?" Erling knocked.

"Hello?" A lady answered, opening the door.

"Hello," He began. "We were just passing through and wondering if you had a place for us to stay. Just for the night if you please."

"Well sure," The middle-aged woman shrugged and welcomed the two into her house. "Husband will be back soon, getting fish from the river, he is."

"Ah," Ezekiel acknowledged. "Quite a cozy house you have yourselves," He sat down at the table in the center of the tiny room.

"Isn't she something? My hubby, Olvir, built it when we first got married. Dwelled here ever since," She admired as worked in the corner fixing tea over the stove. "I'm sure you men will enjoy this later; we have some natural springs just up the hill."

"Hot springs?"

"Oh, yes. Lots of little pools here and there. Great after a long winter's day."

"That sounds lovely, ma'am," Erling smiled as he took a sip from his mug.

"Great catchin' today. Not a single-" A bright, cheerful man walked through the door, seeing strangers in his tiny home. "Well, who's this then?" He smiled.

"Olvir, these men were hiking through the country and needed a place to stay."

"Oh, is that so?" He asked chipperly, as he took off his scarf and newsboy cap. "Where are you all heading then?"

"Reykjavík," Erling said promptly. Zeke chuckled inside, relieved that the old man knew the local geography better than he did.

"Splendid," He smiled. "Hadn't been there for a good number of years. Lovely city. Now, where did you lads say you were from?"

Olvir got tea from his wife, giving her a kiss on the cheek, and sat down.

"Just up in Greenland. Lived there my whole life," Erling nodded. "The young man here's from the States."

"Can't say I've been there. I found myself a remote little nook in the world and decided I was never going to leave," He chuckled. "Ah, it's a dream for me, to be away from all the hustle of city life and to settle down where it's quiet. Living off the land as best we can," They sat in silence for a moment, enjoying their tea, taking in the hand-carved wooden furniture. "Well, why don't we cook up some fish and then we can check out those springs, yeah?"

Olvir and his wife didn't appear to get visitors that often; didn't seem to have any family either. Their enthusiastic hospitality gave that away to the men. Supper was filled with laughter; everyone told stories and grew to understand each other. The cottage was lit by the wood stove and several oil-burning lamps. The homely scene was a warm light in the dark country evening. Even in the most remote corners of the world, the need for human companionship was still truth.

All three of the men let out a sigh after slouching into the hot spring. The pool was constantly heated by the volcanic nature of the island. Zeke looked up to see the stars, bright with the pollutionless skies. The milky way acted as a band of light, watching over the lonely planet. That view was only obstructed by another band. A ribbon of green snaked across the sky.

"Woah," Erling adored. The green aurora was complimented by the fireflies that were also in the fields, blending the heavens with the earth. The lime lightning bugs floated up and formed the stars. Green ribbons in the skies tied the masterpiece together.

Olvir and his wife gave the men some extra clothes for their travels and a leather pack with enough food to sustain them. Ezekiel was pretty sure he was given the wife's old red sweater, but the cotton and wool layers were warm in the cold mornings. They all wished each other farewell and the men were off again. Dew on the ground evaporated into mist, covering the ground in clouds. Into the soft grey, the two men boldly marched.

Clairvoyant

Homeward

On the horizon, a spec grew. Ezekiel and Erling walked onward, as it also drew closer. They had been following the road since the day before last and only now seen their first car. From behind, the vehicle steadily came into shape. The boxy van slowed down as it passed the men, who had their thumbs held up.

"*Góðan dag!*" The young woman rolled down her window.

"Uh, Reykjavík," Erling responded, knowing his limitations in the conversation.

"Reykjavík?" She echoed. They nodded slowly in return. She then put the car into park and gestured toward the back, for them to get in. "*Ég heiti Katla, en þú?*" She turned back to the men, who responded with blank, slightly concerned looks. She realized after a moment they could not understand each other. "Katla," She smiled and put her hand on her chest. She was fit and wore a bright spring dress.

"Ezekiel," Zeke caught on.

"Uh. Erling," The old man introduced himself.

"Reykjavík," She smiled and prompted herself and put the van in gear. The basic commodities of riding in a car, listening to the radio, and feeling the gentle breeze of the air conditioner were nearly lost concepts for Ezekiel. He drifted into a daydream, staring out the window, watching the mountains pass by. He imagined scaling the mountains, canoeing the rivers. If it could be conquered, in his heart, he needed to do it. He needed to test the majesty of Mother Nature; immerse himself into every domain the world held.

Katla talked a little during the ride, presumably about the region they were passing through, but she could have been talking about anything. Neither men paid much attention to her words, but they understood that she may have needed to break the silence with some form of conversation.

"Bless!" She waved goodbye and gave Zeke a wink, as she dropped them off by the bay. The coastal city reflected Nuuk in its colorful buildings but was far greater in population. Above the brightly painted houses, towered a single cathedral in stone white.

"You know she was looking at you more than the road?" Erling nudged.

"So, how do you suggest we get to England from here?" Ezekiel avoided the conversation. The old man laughed.

"Well, can't exactly go through customs. Suppose we could ask some yachtsman, see if they would take us."

"You think they would?"

"I would think so. They're troublesome enough to pick up some hitchhikers and not ask questions. Besides, they're always looking for people to drink with," The old man chuckled from his own founded experience.

"Ahoy, lads!" A well-dressed man called from the deck of his ship.

"Evening," Erling looked back up at him from the pier.

"You men seem lost."

"Aye."

"Well, what can I do you for?"

"Looking to hitch a ride. Wouldn't happen to know anyone with a boat, would ya?" The sailor laughed.

"At the end of the pier, there's a ship called the *Gypsy*. Ask her cap'n. He's the kind of guy that would help ya."

"Thank you," They walked further down and found the ship. It was new and healthy in size. White paint with brightly stained wooden boards.

"Hello?" Ezekiel called. They waited, but only heard the sounds of gulls and waves brushing up. Erling turned and started walking back. "Now where are you off to?"

"Drink. Sailor's intuition," He coughed.

Not far off the docks was a pub. Not a place tourists would go, the Salty Dog was where sailors washed up when in port. It was small;

the concrete building stood alone among the cleats where the ships would dock. Loud, neon beer signs were the only things illuminating the musty building. Seamen, young and old, laughed and clanked steins together. Erling also ordered a pint for himself and Zeke.

"I'll bet you a drink, I can beat you in darts!" Someone called in the background. Erling turned around on the stool and leaned against the bar, taking in the scene and enjoying his beer.

"You bastard, you owe me your ship from last night!"

"Another round o'er here!"

"Afraid not, I won that game of cards. Besides the *Gypsy* won't sail unless her captain's on it," Zeke turned around and looked for the man.

"You lost, now put yer money where yer mouth is, and hand o'er that boat!" The man was in the corner, currently being held up by another drunkard.

"Alright, alright," The skittish man cleared his throat. "If you want her, she's yours."

"Walk me to her then."

"Now?"

"Aye, get up!" The two left, one pushing the other out the door. Ezekiel and Erling set down their glasses and followed behind. The two men in front went away from the pub and down one of the many docks. The captain of the ship took the man to the very end of the pier, walking with his arm around him. They paused for a moment, at the water's edge. Then the captain pushed the man in and ran off. "Bastard!"

"Sorry, lads. No time, I really must run," Erling caught him as he was passing.

"Maybe we can come to an agreement," Erling talked sternly. "You want to run off on your boat and conveniently, we also need a boat to run off in."

"Then what are we doing here?" The captain kept looking over the where he pushed the drunkard in. "She's awaiting."

The *Gypsy* pulled out from port, leaving a soft wake behind it. Faint vulgar words came from a swimmer in the late-night bay. The ship ripped through the ocean, white steel tore through the black water. He steered the ship during the night according to Polaris, preferring to let the stars guide him. Or perhaps he couldn't afford to fix the proper navigational systems for his vessel.

"Morning," The light revealed the captain, still at the helm.

"Morning," Erling nodded back. "Need me to take over?"

"If you wouldn't mind," The old man grabbed the helm as the captain handed it off. He then went for the small fridge and opened a bottle of beer. The captain slouched down in a chair and began taking swigs. "So, what's your cause?"

"Excuse me?"

"You heard me, what's your cause? Why are you needing to get from point 'A' to point 'B'?"

"Just needed to find cheap means of travel and it looked like an opportunity opened up," Erling shrugged. "Preferably without customs."

"Yeah, huh," The young man took another drink. "I know that road. Let's say that's how I get through life. 'Opportunity opened up.' I tend to roll with the punches, but I always end up drifting back out to sea. Guess I'm destined to it!"

"Maybe. Mother Ocean has a way of bringing her sailors back," Erling heard the man scoff.

"Maybe it's just where I always go to run. Tell myself I live a life of piracy and plunder, when I just gamble and drink, coincidentally owning a ship," He sat for a while. "Yeah, I know the road. Always on the run, always escaping the next port town, evading all the sailors I pissed off."

"Sounds like being out here helps you clear your head."

"That or the drinking," He reached for his bottle again. "It's definitely the only place I have left."

The captain was the kind of man who was thrown out of each town he woke up in. He let the alcohol drive him from port to port, searching for something. He was almost waiting for something to happen in his life. Waiting for something to come along and galvanize him, so he kept floating in anticipation.

"I was fiery when he was younger. Filled with sailor's legends and adventure, driven as the waves," The captain looked out to sea. "But then I grew up and shrank into a bottle."

The guiding presence of adventure left him and left behind only a skeleton. His drinks passed straight through and no matter how far he sailed, nothing could fill his hollow corpse. Erling believed most sailors died this way. Long before they're buried, they simply wither from life. Their childhood hopes of being swept into the world dies off.

The two sailors drove the yacht into the morning, over the smooth seas. Erling never caught his name, never bothered to ask either. If the man wanted to live in piracy, then Erling would let him be known as a pirate, the Captain, nothing more to it in his mind. They pressed onward, passed the Faroe Islands and onto Great Britain.

Clairvoyant

The Dispatch

Cikuq and Owen opened the esteemed wooden doors of the Royal Geographical Society building. The antique brick headquarters stood proud with an array of chimneys and white trimmed windows. Mahogany lined the floors and furniture. Dark wooden bookcases were in no short supply, neither were the gentlemen in black suit coats.

"My boys!" An elderly man cried when he saw the two in the threshold of his office. He came and embraced them. "We thought you were deceased," He went to pour out a glass of whiskey for celebration. Cikuq promptly refused.

"Cheers! We were unsure, ourselves, that we'd make it back, sir," Owen began. "And not to diminish our return, but we still have *all* the footage. The, uh, camera was ruined when we were wrecked, but all the film was spared!"

"Excellent, mister O'Donnell, I cannot wait to see what wonders you've captured. Oh, and no worries about the camera, I was going to gift it to you anyway," The elderly man sat back down in his desk, which was decorated with a lengthy nameplate: Director Tobias

Murray, PhD. "I'll have to ring for the rest of your crew to meet back here, they've been anxious about you."

"You son of a-" Aedan stormed into the quiet office and went for Owen. "You stole the film equipment and ran off, you cost us the expedition!"

"Well," The burly man scoffed. "The camera was entrusted to me and never left my possession. Couldn't have stolen it if it were already mine," He sipped his crystal glass of whiskey on ice, then looked to Cikuq for support.

"Also, *you* left us in Greenland, where we were stranded. You called the expedition off," Cikuq added.

"You went all the way to Greenland?" Murray laughed. "All the bloody way over there, that's a splendid little adventure."

"Sir, no disrespect, but we were forced there against our will," Aedan explained.

"Of course, you were forced there. You're explorers for Chrissake, are you not? Hardly ever should you go somewhere on your *own* will."

"Director, you don't seem to understand that these men, my own crew, abandoned the expedition and took with them our supplies. And after one casualty already, we couldn't afford to take any more losses. I'm sure you can sympathize from a leader's perspective that I didn't want to harm anyone else."

"Know your place, boy," Tobias said to the middle-aged man. The room fell silent at Murray's quiet yet powerful words. "Johansson and the rest of the film expedition are under my jurisdiction. Not yours, Aedan. We will not be casting blame on who led the crew astray. You traveled more of the world than you expected, I would call getting lost a success. Now, let's rejoice in the rest of the crew arriving back safely."

"Aye," Owen nodded and stepped out of the office, the others soon filing out.

"Aedan, sit down," Dr. Murray caught him as he was leaving. "You're a poor leader. I need you to be aware of that," Aedan huffed with annoyance. "You need to have some accountability and take responsibility over these things that have happened. You forgot that one of the crew died on this expedition, because you were so puffed up in your own arrogance."

"I don't need to take this," He pushed out from his chair and turned for the door.

"Then we have no more use for you in the Society. Your superiority complex has gotten in the way one too many times," Dr. Murray spoke swiftly. Aedan blew through the door and left an echo quaking throughout the corridors.

"Need a hand with that?" Owen came and asked Dr. Murray, who was attempting to cut and piece strips of film together. The large building was quiet, most people kept to their office, and only rarely left to find one of the countless books in their private collection.

"Figured you went home with everyone else," The Director didn't seem to look up through his bifocals to address the man.

"I spent months on that, there. I wouldn't leave it to be produced in the hands of some amateur," He laughed.

"Very well. Have a seat," The elderly man said. "I was meaning to ask you for help, but you know how stubborn a man's pride can be. Although, now seeing the footage, I am tempted to ask who this man is that you've captured so much of."

"Who, that?" Owen pointed at the frame in Dr. Murray's hand. "That there is Ezekiel Cacheman. The best God damned explorer among us. We found that man when we were in Quebec. Locals were bragging to Aedan about him, so we went and found him. Out of jealousy, of course. 'Zekiel was out there looking for a mammoth. That's the man who led us out of the arctic and saved our hides *and* carried Aedan through a blizzard!"

"Is that so?"

"Every word. You wanted a documentary about life in the arctic circle. I understand that. But that man encompasses everything that adventure and exploration is. Everything the Royal Geographical Society stands for. So, if you want my two cents, sir, I propose we change the angle of our film," Tobias looked down through his glasses and studied the man in the frame. Then he placed the film aside and continued to work on into the evening.

Knocks came barreling through the halls and chambers of the venerated building. Murray looked around from his desk, confused at what was making the disruptive noise.

"I told you, we can just go in. There's no need to knock," Ezekiel was getting irritated with Erling.

"Do you see the sights of this place? There's no way we could walk right in. Too fancy," The scruffy man huffed as he pounded the door again. "They'd have our heads for sure if we got the floors dirty."

"Cheerio, lads," Dr. Murray opened the door as Erling went to pound it again.

"Morning," The two men spoke over each other.

"Can I help you gentlemen?"

"Yeah," Ezekiel jumped in. "We were traveling with a crew of your explorers for some time but, uh, recently separated from them in a shipwreck. We're wondering if they made it back here."

"Step inside," The elderly man opened the door for them, recognizing Zeke from the film.

"Boy!" Owen cried with excitement when the Ezekiel and Erling walked into the office.

"Good to see you, Owen," Zeke gave the man a welcomed hug. "Where's Cikuq?"

"Went home, I'm afraid. Itching to see Canadian soil again, I suppose."

"Glad he made it back safe," Zeke nodded. Owen and Dr. Murray returned their thanksgivings for Ezekiel's arrival. "So, where do we go from here?" Murray smirked at the question.

"Well, the local pub, most likely," The Irishman was quick to holler out.

"No, Owen, what's our next destination? Where do we go next?"

"You want to continue, lad?"

"Well, ya. Why wouldn't we?" He looked around, seemingly lost. It became clear that Ezekiel needed this. He felt like he was losing a part of himself. If there was no drive, he had no purpose anymore. "Why would we not keep going?"

"Young man has a point," Erling leaned back on the desk, stroking his beard.

"You want to continue exploring, Ezekiel?" Dr. Murray asked, intentionally.

"Yes. More than anything."

"Alright. Amen," He went and sat down at his desk. The men looked to each other. "Go. Take whatever supplies you need; we'll get you another camera. Ezekiel, here, has a heart for adventure. Why should we suppress that? The expedition was supposed to last longer anyway."

"Thank you, sir," Zeke went to shake his hand.

"Now get, I believed you left a mammoth over in Canada," Murray shooed them away, laughing.

"You sure you don't need a fourth man?" Aedan caught Ezekiel as he was loading up the van with equipment. No one else was outside in the empty parkway. The London street was relatively quiet in the warm spring day.

"Something tells me we don't work well together," He closed the trunk.

"We may have gotten off on the wrong foot, sure. But none of you are mountaineers. If you plan on going back to Quebec, which you are, you're going to want a guide. You'll need an experienced ice climber."

"I'm sure there are some locals around that would be willing to help out. I know Cikuq wouldn't be far."

"Maybe," He nodded. "Maybe they'll turn you in."

"Are you threatening me, Aedan?" Zeke turned to him.

"No, of course not. I'm being realistic. That's why you didn't stick around to wait for the Coast Guard, right? Didn't want to get put away for years of trespassing?"

"What do you want?"

"Me? Come on, don't make me out to be the bad guy. I'm like you. We both long to travel; we're both explorers," He paused to see Zeke's unimpressed expression. "So, hang me if you will, but we aren't so different. Please, let me come with. I'll step back, but this is all I know. I have no other life outside of the society."

The four men took a ship over to Newfoundland. Aedan kept his distance from Ezekiel and the others. The few days it took to cross the Atlantic, Zeke mapped out where they would begin their search. He marked the village he was originally in, and the estimated location he found the fossil.

As they went north toward Frobisher Bay, they could see the mountains protecting the mainland. The rockface steeped up into the sky, scraping the clouds. Wild grass covered the land, crawling up the sides of the mountains. The green, spring landscape gave way to the stone, which in the heavens, gave way to ice and snow. On the other side of the range was the still water that shown like black glass against the snow. In the city, was a man waiting for the crew to exit the boat.

"Cikuq!" Ezekiel cried. "Glad you were able to join us," He shook his friends' hand.

"Wouldn't miss it."

From the Frobisher Bay, Ezekiel drove northward in the van. Owen had Zeke stop to get footage several times along the way. The giant masses of earth gave the men an appreciation for how small they were. The most holy nature kept men humble.

It would seem that these men had been chosen to wander. Something divine had kept them from planting their feet, kept them on the move. No matter where they were taken in the world, they would always have this guiding presence with them. They had no quarrels with their lifestyle, no ties left that bound them, no societies that restrained them. They were completely and utterly free. Some men explored for the glory, others roamed the world looking to capture it, a very few would set out simply to go where the wind took them.

Ezekiel drove through remote villages, nestled into the foothills and along the shore. They drove far from any known settlement. The valley was relatively flat, which helped their cause, being there wasn't much of a road to follow. Eventually, they made their way back to Kivitoo, the ghost town of a village Ezekiel had lived in. He gave out a sigh of relief to find his house, characteristically untouched. An old axe leaned against the corner near the bunk.

"Alright, so I found the tooth in a pass not far from here," Zeke briefed the men. Aedan leaned against the back wall, disinterested. "I figured we could start there. There's actually an old house up that way that we could base ourselves out of. Erling, you me, and Aedan will take the pass tomorrow. Cikuq and Owen, why don't you go back into the valley and search the lowlands? I'll have a radio that I'll bring up with us and I'll leave one here for you."

The cement floor was cold in the morning. Even through the thick pairs of wool socks, it chilled each foot to the core. They threw on layers over their long-johns and stepped out before the sun could reach them, walking to the base of the mountain with their flashlights to follow. Zeke waved back toward Owen and Cikuq, heading the opposite direction.

"It's a damn crime to have to start the day without coffee," Erling yawned as they began up the trail. The others chuckled at his genuine lament, being tired themselves. Yet they left that all behind them, the occupational hazard of an explorer is being able to get on the move at any hour of the day. So, if that means starting out in the cold, dark morning to get a head start on the trail, so be it.

As the cliffs fell deeper, the stone ridge drove higher. The three men, dwarfed by the size of the arctic mountains, carried on up the dry rock.

They pushed upward as the trail meandered the rugged landscape. There were no trees to provide them with cool shade, the hikers were left in the open heat. They were vulnerable to forces, known and unknown.

"You men go on, I just need to get something," Aedan called ahead to the pair as he was fishing for something in his backpack. They turned and had no problems with gaining some distance from him. A rock shattered to dust in front of the men. A single gunshot echoed off the cliff wall. Shrapnel of stones flew off in all angles.

"Jesus!" They ducked down behind nearby boulders. Aedan was standing further down the bend with a rifle in his hand.

"What the hell?" Ezekiel cried out.

"Bastard," Erling spat. Shots flew over their hideaway. "We can't stay here."

"No, he doesn't have an angle on us. If we continue, we'll be right in his sights."

"Ezekiel!" Aedan hollered again. Zeke kicked several larger rocks off the side of the trail, where the voice echoed from. The boulders rolled down the vertical wall, taking more with them. "I'll kill ya, you bastard! I'll kill you!" Several more shots rang out.

"Help me," Ezekiel commanded as he laid on the ground and continued to push more rubble off the cliff. Erling got down and proceeded to hoist more boulders off the edge. Boulders pounded the cliff as they bombarded down below. The slate broke greater and greater amounts.

"Fuck," The gunman grunted. The ground quaked as the rubble created a movement. A large rockslide began to barrel down toward Aedan. The two ran up the trail, hunched behind the stones. Aedan's leg was caught beneath the crushing boulders, breaking his shin. "Ezekiel!" He screamed in enraged obsession. His heart was filled with jealousy and his mind was poisoned with revenge.

The men ran as soon as they realized there were no more pot shots being taken at them. The trail was steep and gnarled. As much adrenaline as they had, their legs grew weary and their feet began to swell from the pounding on the hard ground.

"Come on, Erling. We can't stop," Ezekiel turned to see his companion collapse onto the shoulder of the rugged trail. "We need to keep moving."

"Okay," He was pulled off the rock and pressed up the earthy stairs again. They trudged onward into the day. Fear pursued them, they reluctantly dragged themselves forward, up the mountainous terrain. They fled further away from their enemy, yet also grew further away from help.

"They won't have their radio on them until night, when they're back in the house," Zeke grunted as he walked. "Even then, if we call them, there isn't much they can do," Zeke thought aloud.

Night crept in, covering the mountains in darkness. As the sun blackened, the men grew continuously worried.

"Do we stop?" Erling turned about, once total blackness set in. "Ezekiel?" Ezekiel kept walking up the trail that could no longer be seen.

"Son let's rest here for the night," Erling called, staying back.

"This was my fault," Ezekiel stopped.

"What?"

"I got us into this. Aedan wants me," Zeke turned and started back down the trail. "If I go down, he'll only kill me and then no one else would have to get hurt. He would be satisfied."

"No," Erling clenched Ezekiel's arm as he went by. "You're not going back down there. You don't need to sacrifice yourself."

"I don't need anyone else to die because of me," He ripped away. "You go over the pass and get to safety."

"I said no, boy!" Erling hollered. "I won't let you die. If someone died at your hands, then let that be. I don't much know what you've done, but I know what we can do right now," The old man walked to the silhouette. "Don't do this," He spoke sternly. "I am not leaving you. Do you understand? You're not giving into him."

"Okay," Zeke took off his pack and nestled into the rocks. Hoping to find safety and rest away of the trail.

The next morning came and the men packed up in silence and moved further into the mountain.

"What do you we think?" The two men peered behind boulders, at a wooden house that was built on the hillside. The silent building that Ezekiel foretold appeared abandoned. The windows were dark and there were no traces of anyone.

"He could be in there," Erling whispered. "I don't like the looks of it."

"You think he could have passed us in the night?" Zeke asked. "He might have gotten hurt in the landslide.

"If he hasn't given up already," Erling speculated. "We weren't shot at after we got away."

"No," Ezekiel shook his head. "If he was driven enough to follow us all the way out here and wait until we were alone, he will be driven enough to finish the job. This wasn't impulsive, he planned this out and will continue to pursue us until the end."

"Damn," Erling coughed. "I'll check and see if he's in there," Ezekiel put his hand on Erling's shoulder, but the old man made his way back to the trail. The sound of his faint steps was carried throughout the still land. Erling slowly approached the dark building. He paused as he went up to the door. He looked back at Zeke before stepping into the shadow of the house.

He waited in silence for several minutes. Not a sound came from the house. The door remained opened as it was left, allowing the watchman to see into the blackness inside. Zeke sat in horror, neglecting to respond to anything around him. His face was flushed of color and his eyes looked as if he was rewatching the most painful memory of his life.

"He's in there," Ezekiel finally exhaled and slouched back behind the rocks, turning away from the scene. "God save me," He wiped his eyes with his palm. His stomach was caving in, hollowing out his body. Zeke stepped out from behind the rocks and walked down to the house.

The glass was full of black grime and the log walls had withered from years of brutal weather, carved from passing ice. Zeke's head became light, barely keeping his balance. His steps grew heavier as he got to the threshold. He pushed open the heavy wooden door. Through the faint dawn light and the gentle fire in the hearth, Erling's body was illuminated on the ground.

"God," Ezekiel trembled. Tears fell from face as he quivered in disbelief. He stepped back out of the house and fell onto the wall.

Out of the black interior, the barrel of a rifle slowly came into the light, with Aedan's panicked hands. He peered out front, not checking around him. Ezekiel grabbed the barrel of the gun and punched Aedan from his blindside. He pulled the trigger, but the fall of the hammer led to nothing.

Aedan recovered and beat Zeke with the stock of his gun. Zeke tackled him into the wall. Aedan punched Ezekiel off of him and limped inside on his broken leg. Zeke flung the door back open and staggered in. A burning log hit him over the head. As the man was building himself back up, Aedan hit him again. Zeke pulled on his attacker's ankles, tripping Aedan into the fireplace. Flames caught his jacket on fire, which he quickly discarded.

"You took everything from me!" Aedan screamed as he put his fists up. His face was dirty from ash and sweat and his leg was still seeping blood.

"You killed him," Zeke muttered. "You took this too far!"

"No! No, you replaced me! You undeserving swine. I deserve to be remembered! I've gone farther than you ever will! I'll be remembered with Percy Fawcett and Robert Peary, one of the greats! *The greatest.* You'll all die out here and fade into history, tragic accidents for the sake of discovery."

"Was that worth all of this?" The fire began to ignite along the floorboards, slowly branching out from the jacket and scattered logs. "You can have it. You can be the world-renowned explorer, take all the credit for everything I've done, add it to your achievements! Go find the stupid thing. That doesn't matter to me! But you," Zeke began to tear up. "You killed Erling! No one had to die."

"It isn't enough, Ezekiel! As long as you're alive, I could never have that glory. You woke up the wrong giant! There can only be one in this game! No one will remember you, but only if you all disappear!" He screamed into the smoky air. "You woke up the wrong giant!"

"You're demented," Zeke cried. "You're insane!" Aedan charged at him and brought Ezekiel to the ground. He wrapped his hands around Ezekiel's neck and violently slammed up and down. Zeke was kicking and hitting the man with whatever strength he had. He found a log and rammed it at Aedan's head. Zeke hurled over in relief, gasping for air, which was getting notably thinner. He hadn't realized the piece of wood he grabbed was completely consumed in fire. The flames engulfed the walls and burned holes in the ceiling. Zeke clenched his burnt hand as he ran for the door. He hesitated, not wanting to leave Erling behind. The second story of the house caved through the ceiling.

"No!" Zeke screamed. He fell backwards, out of the house, then scrambled to get some distance. "Oh God," He wept. The fire ate the house, consuming everything on the lonely mountainside. The smoke rose a ways, but then dissipated into the clouds not far above.

Zeke started to hyperventilate. The yellow fire reflected off of the tears swelling up. He ran up the mountain.

Clairvoyant

Redemption

The echo of footsteps could have easily been mistaken for the rumble of a glacier as it creaks and moves. Not even the wind above the clouds could overtake the sound of marching. The man who scaled up the mountain, eventually turned and began to hyperventilate again.

"I don't understand," He repeated to himself, shaking his head. "I don't understand. I don't understand," He began pulling on his hair, rocking his crippling body. "I don't understand!" He screamed into the clouds. The echoes faded away with the wind.

"Come on! Kill me already!" He taunted. "Just kill me already," He collapsed into the snow. "Why-I don't-why would you do this to me? Why would you curse me like this? Why would you create my life, just have it bring death? I don't get it, Lord. I don't understand. Why bring me here? Why would you kill everyone I love? What are you trying to prove?!" He screamed into the wind.

"You took everything from me," The more he cried, the emptier he felt.

"I hate- I hate how everything around me is ruined. God, I hate...
It's all because of Lane... I'm reminded of him every time I see the
snow. My best friend died on Christmas day because of me. Don't
know if you remember that," He began to speak more slowly.

"I survived, but he lost his life. You killed him and let me live
on. And all because I was young. I wanted to conquer the world that
I thought was promised to me. I thought you blessed those who
followed you. I don't understand why you would put me through
this," Ezekiel paused and let more tears run down and freeze on his
face. He took a deep breath before continuing.

"Winter's nothing to me but death. I see only the blood in the
snow. I can't sleep without seeing him, God. It haunts me! I can't
even look at myself without seeing judgment written on me. And
now- I knew one day I'd have to pay for the sin of getting him killed,
only then would you finally finish me off. So, let's have it then!
Haven't you put me through enough? How much more do you need
me to endure, God?!" He threw around the snow he was sinking in.

"You drove me out into exile, forbid to come back home. Never
once could I return because of what I committed. I swore, I knew I
would die out here in the wilderness! I thought that I was abandoned
and ripped away from you're your grace, cursed by my own stupid
sins!"

Zeke sniffed up a few more tears and wiped away his runny nose.
"But you know what I realize, despite all of this?" He began again.

"That I was no longer being carried away. I ran so far away from home that I realized I was starting to run toward something else. That no one was chasing me… I was running towards redemption. Having a purpose again reminded me that life goes on," He paused, starting to understand. "I needed to forgive myself and I think I hadn't done that before. I think I needed to realize that you had forgiven already me, hadn't you? God, I was so consumed with myself. I was so depressed, I forgot who I was."

Ezekiel turned his head, panning across the great view of clouds rolling softly over each other, meeting the heights of the mountains with gentle vapor. The ice on the ridge shone like opal, reflecting off of the ethereal light dispersed from the atmosphere. Silver covered the ground below. And flowing rivers from melting snow, roared softly into the deep valley, filling all the trees below with life. Ezekiel put his face to the ground and began to weep.

"No, you didn't do this to me. You made something out of it. I saw the world. I sailed over seas and climbed mountains, chased myths and met mighty men," Zeke lifted himself up. "And even winter. Winter is so beautiful; I mean, even the cold wind is your Spirit. You dwell in places like this," Zeke started to shake his head in awe, still trying to suck up tears.

"I used to think it was all dead, but winter isn't death. It's so, so peaceful… God, I realized that you didn't abandon me in exile. You didn't leave me for my mistakes. You came with me. You were there. You *are* here," Ezekiel exhaled, slowing himself to the stillness of the world around him. The top of the vast and glorious mountain range surrounded Ezekiel in white and blue. He closed his eyes and felt the wind against him.